The Dead Notebook

BY
CHUCK SINGLETON

The Dead Notebook

Written By

Chuck Singleton

Book design and cover art by and ©Chuck Singleton. All rights reserved.

The Dead Notebook is ©2019 Chuck Singleton. All right reserved. No parts of this story may be reproduced without express written permission from the copyright holder. The Dead Notebook, all contents, and distinctive likenesses thereof are Copyright ©2019 Chuck Singleton. This is a work of fiction. Any similarities between actual or fictional persons, institutions, living or dead without satiric intent is purely coincidental. All characters created by Chuck Singleton and Mitch Shelman.

To: General Thomas Samuels
Joint Chiefs of Staff
United States Army

From: General Thaddeus Morganstein
Department of Defense
United States Marine Corp

Top Secret Information. Eyes Only

    We have successfully sealed the borders on all sides of the state of Washington due to the outbreak of the Dead Animating Virus (known from here forward as the D.A.V.). Our office has pinpointed where the outbreak began in the small southwest Washington town of Winlock. We discovered the laboratory in the town under the supervision of Darbus Mentler, former biologist and pathologist of the C.D.C. We believe he synthesized the virus at this lab, under the authority of Lt. General Carlton Reginald, of Joint Base Lewis/Mchord.
    His whereabouts are currently unknown.
    Under the direction of the General, Mentler created the D.A.V. for a biological weapon of undetermined purposes. Mentler was released from the C.D.C. for ethical violations and unlawful human testing. General Reginald, we feel, recruited Mentler after his termination.
    Tom, this is being treated as a domestic terrorist attack, and Reginald is being charged with treason. The President is very aware of this and is extremely unhappy with this situation. He has given us 24 hours to coordinate and get an operation to apprehend both men. If they are even still alive.
    Included are note books we've code named the "DEAD NOTEBOOK". It has been copied and transcribed from written accounts of what occurred to those involved found in the eastern part of Washington State. There are dates in it to show the chronology of what the people went through in Winlock, and as it stretched across the state. We have found other journals and video recordings, and have teams studying them. They will be reproduced soon, but the priority is finding these two individuals.

    My office will be contacting yours within 12 hours to begin planning.

Major General Thadeous Morganstein,
D.O.D., United States Marine Corp

May 15

This writing is to chronicle the end. The virus, bacteria, or whatever it is making the dead walk, is unknown. Is it biological? A terrorist weapon? Is it from outer space? No one knows. All we know, is dead people are rising. I saw the symptoms on my cousin, just before he died and then tried to eat me. Yes, eat me. He had blood coming out of every orifice on his body.

Not everyone looks like they're affected by this whatever. Those that are immune, though I think it is just a matter of time before the rest of us get it, or became dinner for the ones who are infected.

Deaders.

That's what I'm calling them.

The deaders are feeding on people and animals if they are alive. I watched a group of deaders rip apart a pit bull, and the only thing left was part of its jaw bone. They heard, then saw an old woman coming out of her house yelling for her husband or whoever. She lasted less than ten minutes, if that long. The more she screamed, the more deaders came at her. I didn't know her, but still……

All that was left of her was her left hand. Or rather her thumb, palm, and two fingers.

I don't know if it is just happening here in Winlock, Washington, or anywhere else. This might be state wide, or even all over the world. Maybe, just maybe it is a test from God. Where only the strong survive? I guess. I hope. I think the human race will make it. I'm recording this so anyone who finds this will maybe know how to beat this. Fight it. Something. I just hope this doesn't get repeated.

As I write this, I'm upstairs of this house looking out the window toward the center of town. There is a swarm of deaders outside the house, trying to get in. Some have. I can hear them outside the door of the room I'm in. I tried to seal the door, but it isn't going to last long. I'm throwing this note book out the window inside this backpack with the hope that someone will find it and read it. Whoever finds this, record how you're surviving. People need to know.

I have to go now. I'm throwing this out the windo

May 25

It took me 3 days to get to this house. I was only a block away, hiding out in a shop. Every time I tried to walk outside, I was almost surrounded by these creeps. Or "deaders" as the note book says. I don't know where they were hiding, but they just came out of nowhere when I opened the door. They must hear really good.

I never ran so hard in my life when I finally got out of the shop. As I ran, I jumped and kicked some deader girl so hard that her head came completely off. She was decaying so badly; I'm surprised she didn't fall apart walking down the street!

So I run pass this house and find this backpack with the note book in it. It's telling whoever finds it to record everything they can, so here I am writing as much as possible. I rest for a time. The only reason I'm able to is because the deaders lose interest if you get to far from them, thank God. Some of them keep following you until they hit a wall. Literally. I think the ones that follow you for a long ways are the ones that are freshly…..I don't know. I guess dead. But, I noticed if there are a bunch of them doing something, they just make more of them come see what's going on. Must be the noise.

My luck just ran out. I'm in this small house that has like a zillion windows, and it wasn't boarded up very well. I know some of them saw me come in, and I am hiding out in this bedroom. Suddenly there is a super-loud crash. A window, has to be. I'm going to throw this out and hope someone gets to it. There goes the door to the room. I'm done.

May 26

      I just watched my neighbor Thomas attack his wife. Their granddaughter had come running out of the house screaming when she saw what was happening. She didn't get far. Horrible.

      My husband Karl, son K.J, and myself are hiding in our attic. I came down to check the neighbors because we lost track of them when everything went to hell. I couldn't see them, but when I did, I was glad they didn't see me. Thank goodness we can pull up the ladder to the attic. We've been hiding out for at least 7 days, and I have never seen K.J. so quiet.

      After I saw what Thomas did to his wife Ellen, and watching the little girl, I am still shaken by that. I saw the backpack that she'd dropped. Her screaming drew more and more to her. I'm hoping whoever finds this, lets the world know what is happening here. Unless, of course, the world is gone.

I better get back to the boys. They are probably worried.

      Please, whomever finds this, give to the proper authorities. This madness needs to end.

                                        Alanis Curtane

May 30

	Found this stupid notebook and backpack on the ground. I didn't think there was still stupid people alive. I went into this house to see if I could find something to eat, and all I found was this stupid thing. Checked the cupboards, bedrooms, and stuff but there was nothing. Everything is empty. The stupid bitch that wrote in this stupid notebook is probably dead. Because she's stupid.
	Going through people's yards is a good idea. The stupid deaders are staying mostly to the street. Sometimes, I come across one. Then I hit its stupid head off with my baseball bat! These things smell like my stupid grandma's house bathroom! Nasty.
	I come up on this convenience store. It's owned by a stupid gook family. They tried to bust me for lifting a half case of Miller, but they failed. Stupid gooks. He told me to never come back. He can kiss my ass.
	I don't see anyone in here, so I'm going to hang for a while. Still some food in here which is good. These guys are such tight wads. Their prices are too high, and some of it is expired. Stupid gooks, I hope they are all dead.

	I thought I heard something in the cooler. I

May 30

I shot the boy. We heard him coming toward the cooler, and I did not know if he was one of the living or one of the creatures. This is the same boy that tried to steal from us a few weeks ago. I didn't like him, but I certainly didn't want to kill him. I am going to the store front and lock the door. The family is in the back so I better hurry. Nothing else inside, but that doesn't mean something won't try to get in.

Good. Store is empty and I got the door shut and locked. I need to get back to the cooler. It is starting to get dark and I will feel much safer, and so will my family. I hope this ends soon.

May 31

We made it through another night. My oldest boy is getting restless and wants to try and get something from our house like his books or DS. I don't know. I told him it is too dangerous. We may live just behind the store, but just outside is 20 or 30 of the dead ones walking around right in the alley behind us. He is upset, but I hope he understands that his things are not worth it. I need to check the front of the store, make sure we are still secure.

The doors are still locked, and no sign of broken glass. That's good. Then my wife screams. I run to check on her and find out our oldest left! And his little sister followed! I tell the wife to stay here.

I find my daughter. Or what's left of her. Why? Why disobey me? She didn't even make it to the fence. I am going in to get him.

He didn't make it either. The house is overwhelmed by the dead things I have to go back to the store. Then I notice the door to the back is open! Oh my god! My wife! The dead are everywhere!

June 3

    My name is Collin Jensen. I found this backpack and note book next to Mr. Kim, or more appropriately what was left of him. He owns the convenience store right in the middle of town. Looking at the state of him, I'm thinking his entire family is gone. Yep, there is what's left of his daughter. I met them at an event at the high school where I teach. Their oldest son is quite the wrestler. I can only imagine where the rest of the family is. I see the back door of the store is open, I think I'll check it out. I'm almost certain, about 99.99999% ad infinitum, he won't mind.

    Inside the store isn't so bad. Oh. I found what is left of his wife. Man, what the fricking dead heads did to her is pretty disgusting. Luckily, the store is pretty empty of any deaders, and there is still some food on the shelves. A long with some other necessities. I think I'll find a way to secure the building and call it day. I'll move out tomorrow. I found batteries and even a flashlight. Cool. I guess I better close it up; the deaders seem to come out a lot more at night.

June 4
Collin's Notes

Made it another night. Never know if and when I won't. I better move on and try to get to the city limits and look for help. I ran into another survivor today. I helped him get away from about 6 deaders. It was going really well until I caught him trying to get into my backpack. I yelled at him and he pulled a 6inch hunting knife on me. We started fighting and he cut me, but not too bad. We both went down fighting for the knife, and I was able to smack his head on the ground. He dropped the knife and I grabbed it. He was screaming and cussing as I backed away from him.
The idiot didn't notice the 5 or 6 deaders coming up behind him. We were pretty noisy.

He began to yell even louder when the first deader grabbed him and bit his shoulder. Then he was really screaming and that brought even more of them. So I ran, and by the time I was far enough away to feel safe about stopping and looking back, there had to be at least 20 of the creeps going at him like a pack of cheetahs tearing up a gazelle. Good. The guy was dick.

Getting dark. I better find a safe place before I become an item on the menu myself.

June 5

Seems like there are more and more deaders every day. I saw the Thompson family cutting between houses. They lived right across the street from us. The wife's and my first house. The worst part about this? I watched her attack our dog and rip its throat out with her teeth. I knew then what I had to do. I know I did her a favor when I put her down with the electric hedge trimmer, but it still doesn't make me feel any better. Till death do us part doesn't take into account if either of us is "undead".

There goes the Thompsons again. I think I'll go get them. This house I'm in is pretty secure, and maybe together we can help each other and get out of here.

I got them. Jim and I nailed more boards up over the windows. His wife Lana isn't handling this very well. She keeps wanting to "protect" the 3 kids, but the way she wants to do that is completely different than how I think anyone else would do it. She has this big carving knife that she is actually playing with, and not in a safe way. She must have cut herself a half a dozen times! Jim is doing the best he can with her, but I can see the kids getting a little nervous around her. I'm a little concerned.

We start to settle down for the night, and they all decide to give me my own room. I understand them feeling safer if I'm not there in the same room with them. They may think I might do the same thing that jerk wad tried to do to me. That's fine, I'd do the same. On that note, I'm not sure I can trust Lana.
Before I go to sleep, I'm going to figure a way to lock this door of the room I'm in.

June 6

Jim and Lana's 3 kids are tough. The 8-year-old, Kyle, doesn't really understand what's happening, I think. But I'm pretty sure he's smarter than any of the rest of us would consider. I should remember that since I teach at the high school. If any of us get through this' it will be him. Jess and Tara, the girls, I've been watching them and they are scared. Tara is only 13 but she is smarter than half the grown-ups I've come into contact with in this area.

The 15-year-old Jessica, everyone calls her Jess, is trying so hard to help the other 2. All 3 of them see their mom losing it. I overheard Jess tell her dad that she walked in on her mom cutting herself and rambling on about making all of them safe.

We've been in this house for almost 2 days. The way Lana is acting, I'm worried that we may not make it to 3.

June 7

I went looking for Jim this morning to get him and his family moving on and he screamed. I ran to where he and Lana were sleeping and she had cut his hand off. "The only way we'll be safe, "she says, "is when we're all dead!" She plunged the knife into Jim's eye and he falls over lifeless. She started charging me, swinging the knife back and forth. I dodged her as she came at me and she faced planted herself on the floor outside the room. I quickly jumped on her back and held her down, getting the knife out of her hand and tossing it away. While I had her pinned she kept screaming, "We need to be safe! We need to be safe!" I asked about the kids, and all Lana said is that they are safe. I don't want to know any more. Suddenly, there is shuffling behind me and it is Jim! My God he's a mess. He lunges at me and I move, but Lana doesn't. She screams as he tears a piece of flesh from her neck with his teeth.

I grab what I can and get out. Lana's screams draw more deaders to the house. They ignore me to go for her. Like I could stop them if I wanted to. I learned one thing though. Whatever is causing the dead to rise isn't necessarily from being bitten. I think it is airborne.

June 8

I'm not sure what the date actually is. I think it's the 8, but I'm just going by the calendar I found since I don't have my watch. This has been with me longer than anyone else who's used it. Still, going to be a while to get out of town. I don't know if this is only happening here or not. I hope not.

I can't stop thinking about the kids. The wife and I talked about having some before everything went to hell in a hand basket. This really, really sucks. I miss her. What's that? I see a flash light moving in a house not far from where I'm at. I'm going to check it out.

It's the kids! I found the kids! I don't know how thy made it, but I'm so happy I could crap my pants. The only thing I can ask them is how? Their mother said they were "safe" and that meant dead. Jess saw what was happening and got the other two out. Tara wrote a suicide note telling them they didn't want to live in this world. I guess Lana found it. I told you she was smart. They got out, which I told them was probably one of the bravest and stupidest things anyone could have done.
Then comes the question I was dreading. They want to know about Jim and Lana. I tell them they are gone, but I don't tell them how. They cry and I try to comfort them. But I remind them they're safe, and I'm going to do everything I can to keep them that that way.

June 10

Been a couple of days. These 3 kids are amazing! Tara, when she was digging around the house found a stash of firecrackers, roman candles and a bunch of pop bottle rockets. The kids and I are going to come up with a plan and utilize them to get out of here. The city limits are only about 3 or 4 miles from where we are, but they may as well be 3 or 4 thousand. Looking out the window, there has got to be a zillion deaders milling about. I didn't think Winlock had that many people living here.

Kyle came running in all excited. He found 2 shot guns and 4 full boxes of ammo. Got to love rural Lewis County with all the hunters and rednecks. Got a gun in every house!

Not really.

June 11

We're doing a test run with the fireworks. The bottle rockets whistle and then pop at the end so I'm going to sneak out as far from the house I can and light at least 2. 25 yards should do it. Pretty sure I can make it back. Here goes nothing.

It worked. I launched 2 just to be sure and its whistling drew the deaders to where it landed, then popped. And that brought more to it. Looked like all but a few stragglers went for it. Good! Thank God, I think we're going to be able to do this!

June 12

Today is the day. I looked outside to where the rockets landed and we've come up with another plan. The kids are scared, but I believe they know that this is our best option. They are going to wait just outside the door, Jess with one of the shot guns. I have the other and all the rounds. I showed her how to load it and fire, reminding her about the recoil. I living in a rural town, knowing how to use a gun isn't all bad. But who thought I'd need it to fight off a bunch of zombies. So, I light 3 rockets and they launch away from us. I told the kids to pack just we needed, but make it light. We need to move as fast as possible. I then light some fire crackers with an extended fuse to hopefully draw them here away from where we are running. Here goes.

We get 6 blocks away. We get to an apartment building, but there are about 50 deaders around and I don't want to use the gun. It will just bring more. We find an open place with 2 bedrooms on the second floor and decide this is as good a place as any to stay. All the kids help barricade the stairs so we should be safe. For now. I'm glad we didn't use the guns. That might have just made getting here a lot harder.

Dark out now. I'm going to try to get up on the roof and get a lay of the land. We might just get out of here tomorrow.

June 13

I made a humungous screw up. We back tracked 6 blocks farther away from the edge of town. We might as will be on another planet! We're going to have to stay here for a while. I'm not sure how long though. We do have a problem that might become serious. Our food supply is getting low. There are other apartments near us so I guess we'll have to scavenge a bit. There are homes close by, but about 50 to 60 yards away. And I don't like the looks of the undead population. I might get to one, but I might not get back. If we're careful, we should be able to stretch the food a day or two. Maybe.

I better let Jess and the others know the bad news.

June 14
Jess notes

Collin left the note book so I decided to add my two cents worth. My name is Jessica Thompson (Jess for short). I'm the oldest of three kids at 15. Tara is 13 and our little brother Kyle is 8. Collin told us the mistake he made, and we told him it is alright. He is keeping us safe and together. Since it is just us now. I saw what happened to mom and dad. I don't think I'm going to tell the other two. At least not until we're safe.

Before he left, Collin gave Tara and I a reminder about the shotgun and how to use it. I don't think Tara is too excited about it, but as long as I know we should be good. Kyle wanted to learn, but Collin said no. He thinks if Kyle fired it, he could get hurt just by the recoil. But he did promise to show him some time.

It's been a few hours and Collin isn't back yet. Kyle keeps watching for him. I told him Collin might not make it back until tomorrow, but he wants to keep watch in case he needs help. He is so cute. There have only been a few deaders out there since he left, but it is starting to get dark.

Please, God, keep Collin safe.

Collin got back just as it got dark. He found two gallons of distilled water, full, and like three boxes of Pop Tarts. Kyle was really happy about the tarts. It is nice to see him smile. I give Collin back the note book and told him I saw what happened with mom and dad. He apologizes that he couldn't do anything for them, and he almost cries. I hug him and tell him its fine. He is keeping us safe and together with him. It is more than we could ask for.

I hope he doesn't see this, but I sure liked hugging him. I hope we get to do it again.
And again.

June 15
Collin's notes

    I couldn't ask for a better group of kids! Kyle is always asking if he can help, and the girls are just amazing! Everyone is just really coming together. I wish my students did this. Jim and Lana raised them right. I actually got lucky today and found some Spaghettios. It's weird though. A lot of places have power in them. I guess the infrastructure is still working. But for how long? Anyways, the kids are happy that they can eat something different than Pop Tarts. Kyle loves these things. I don't hate them, but I prefer the real thing. The kids are smiling and that's good enough for me.

    Jess told me she saw the note about her parents. I thought that maybe they wouldn't even try to look for it, but I'm not surprised. The priority was getting supplies and stuff. She apologized, but I told her it was fine. She also said that she wouldn't tell the other 2 about their parents until we are safe. She's a great kid. Smarter and more mature than I was when I was her age. Something else about her too.

Stop it! She's a kid.

    Tomorrow we make a plan to get out of here. I'm climbing on the roof and picking a direction. I will get these kids to safety. No matter what.

June 16

We were woken up by the sound of gunfire right at daybreak. Tara was the first one to see what was going on. She thought it was the military. Nope. 3 guys found some guns and the liquor store. Not good.

They were about a block away when one of them spotted her through the window. I'm not going to repeat what they said, but I am ready to kill them! She ran back to the rest of us shaking and crying. Jess hugged her and Kyle was up and ready to put down anyone trying to hurt his sister.

We could hear them getting closer. The idiots are so flipping loud they're going to bring every deader for a thousand miles! I think I can get us out of here through the sliding glass door by climbing down the balcony.

Not going to work. Too many deaders are right outside in the back. Probably the gun shots drew them. Jess just screamed. One of the guys is on our level. She saw him walk by, so I give her one of the shot guns and move them to a bedroom. I let her know that if they don't hear my voice on the other side of the door, shoot.

A bullet whizzes by my head. My gun is ready and pointed at the door. He kicks it in and I fire at him from about 3 feet away. His right arm separates from his body, and he screams when he falls backwards over the railing. His friends come running firing their guns wildly. Biggest and last mistake they'll ever make. I yell for the kids to bring me some firecrackers. I want to add fuel to the fire, so I light them and throw them at the guys. Suddenly, the combo of crackers and gun fire brings so many deaders out I can't even count them. They shoot, bringing even more. Soon, the two of them are overwhelmed and drown in a sea of the undead. Serves them right.

We are able to climb down the back after all the noise. The few we run into are easily avoided. We finally make it to a house that is pretty secure and finally relax, if you can call it that.

The kids calm down and I take the time to realize what I had done. I killed a man. I start to cry and Jess comes in. She figures out why I'm doing that, and she puts her arms around me. "You did what you had to do to save us," she whispers. I hug her back, still in tears. It is nice. The other 2 come in and pretty soon all of us are hugging.

I honestly don't know what I'd do without Jess.

And the other 2, too.

June 19
Collin's notes

Been a few days since I've recorded. Sometimes I just want to get through this and not worry about chronicling, but people need to know. Maybe, just maybe, this won't happen to anyone else. If anyone is still alive. I do have to say that this is therapeutic. I'll keep writing as long as I can.

This place we found is pretty good spot to collect ourselves and get our bearings. Even found some food and water in the basement of the house. The kids are tired and ready to stay for a while. I agree, but just to get rested. It will only be safe for so long. They'll think about their parents and break down, but that's good. It will hopefully help them come to terms with everything else.

We need to get the hell out of here, and I haven't a clue on how we're going to do it.

June 20

I need to find a pharmacy or doctor's office. Tara has a fever and it is pretty high. She is confused, can barely talk, and when she tries to stand she falls back down. Thank God this house had some Tylenol, but it can only do so much. Jess is staying by her, and Kyle is doing "guard duty ". It will hopefully keep him occupied while I figure something out.

Got to love this town. I found a nine millimeter with tons of ammo in this house. I'm going to let Kyle carry it, but not before I teach him how to handle it safely. I'm heading out, and I want them safe. Jess is going to be with Tara, and I don't know if she will be able to defend the house. Kyle is smart, and I know he'll do everything he can, but he is still an 8-year-old boy. I take a quick look at him and chuckle. He has his chest out, kind of marching around with one hand one the gun in his pocket. He'll be the best guard ever.

From one of the upstairs rooms, I can see a store and a possibly an RX on the side. Guess I better start working on a plan to get to it. Then come up with a back-up plan for that and about 8000 contingency plans to cover those.

Oh boy.

Jess' notes

Collin left to go get the medicine. I can see the store from upstairs. It is maybe 6 or 7 blocks away, and all the deaders are on the street. None of them are seeing him behind the houses so that's good. He took a baseball bat he found and one of the shot guns. I pray he doesn't need the gun. As he was leaving I watched him hit the head off of a deader. It was pretty disgusting.

Tara's fever went down, thankfully. She's talking and asking for water, which means she is probably getting her appetite back. Collin is still gone. I know it has only been a couple of hours, but still. I'll start worrying when it gets dark.

Kyle came running up to me all excited. He said he saw a group of about 12 people running from house to house. I looked and he was right. One of them started to look our way and I grabbed him and pulled him out of view. He got irritated and started getting tough and wanted to know why. I told him, "We don't know about them. They could be nice, or they could come in here and take what we have and hurt us. Or worse." He said he was sorry and went back to his guard duty. I guess that could've been worse.

All of us were startled to the sound of firecrackers outside. I peeked and saw the deaders walking toward the noise. Collin came running like an Olympic athlete around the opposite side where the creeps were, and he had a bag of stuff. He tripped! And there's a deader almost right on top of him! He's not going to be able to get out of the way! Collin rolls to one side as the zombie face plants right next to him, except it's between him and the house. Both of them get off the ground at roughly the same time. The deader lunges at Collin and gets ahold of his shirt. The deader snaps at him trying to get a mouth full, but Collin is able to knock him down and start booking it toward the house. I think he lost the shot gun because I don't see it with him. I better get to the door and let him in.

He has all kinds of medicine in the bag. Anti-biotics, morphine, all types. Thank God he is safe. I don't know what I'd do without him.

I mean what *we'd* do without him.
But mostly me.

June 21
Collin's notes

Tara's fever finally broke. She's eating and doing an excellent job of keeping everything down. That is a good thing because I hate other people's puke.

I think I may have found a way out of here. I need to investigate more and probably be gone a few days. When I was getting the medicine at the store I thought I saw some military guys walking around. I made sure they couldn't see me because they could've been some whack-jobs dressed in camos. Looked like maybe 5 or 6. I let the kids know what I saw and what I think we should do. Jess isn't happy because I'm planning to go alone. I tell her it will be safer for them, and I'll be able to move quicker. This way they can board up the house, and stay relatively safe. Jess runs off in tears and the other 2 get worked up. I let them know I plan to be gone no more than a day or two. They know I want nothing more than to get them out of this hell-hole any way I can. I ask them to sit tight so I can go talk to Jess.

I find her sitting and still crying. I sit next to her and put my arm around her. She responds by turning and hugging me like she is never going to see me again. I tell her nothing is going to stop me from getting back to her and getting her out of here.

And the other kids too.

June 22

I'm heading out in a couple of minutes. Jess is still upset, but feeling better after our talk last night. Tara is up moving around now, so she and Kyle decide to secure the house a little bit more. The kids are awesome! The way they pull together and work. If the wife and I had had kids, I would love them to be like these 3.

I decide to leave Jess the guns. The main reason is I'd hate to lose any more fire arms. So I've got the bat and I also found a machete in the basement. It's in pretty good shape. I have a back pack, the weapons, and a little food and water to tide me over for the time I'm gone. I hope I don't run out, but maybe I'll find more.

I got us turned around and heading the wrong way. But I think Napavine is just a couple miles away. We might be able to get out of here that way. Well, I'm sure as hell going to try.

I got 2 blocks away when I had to duck in to this shack. It's about 6 feet by 12 feet, so it might be a little uncomfortable. I check and make sure I brought some firecrackers. Yep. I did. Might need to make a break for it. There is a huge flock of deaders about 10 yards from where I'm at. I don't think I can make it without something to distract them. I light and throw some. Here goes.

It works. I find a bigger place to hunker down for the night, and it is a lot safer.

Before I left, I gave the kids some notebooks I found at the store so they can do their own writing. I let them know that it is important to keep it up in case I can't any more. Saying that went over like a fart in church. They didn't like it at all.

To: General Thomas Samuels
Joint Chiefs of Staff
United States Army

From: General Thaddeus Morganstein
Department of Defense
United States Marine Corp

      Some of the following excerpts were found by personnel on a search and rescue for more survivors. After careful research of the materials, we believe these recordings were made by the children who accompanied Collin Jensen. The narrative has been inserted somewhat chronologically to understand better what happened during this particular time.
      There is evidence that one of the children is still alive. But there is no way of knowing her whereabouts at this time.

Major General Thadeous Morganstein,
D.O.D., United States Marine Corp

June 22
Jess' notes

Collin left. He gave us notebooks to record on so we can best describe what's happening. He found us extra food and water, so our supply is good until he gets back. We also have the shotgun and pistol, but I don't feel safe.

My biggest concern is keeping Tara and Kyle safe. I'm not sure I can do it alone. I know Collin only left ten minutes ago, but I already miss him and I'm scared to death for him. I have no idea why I'm feeling what I'm feeling for him. He's like 25 or 26 and I'm just 15. Maybe it is the situation we're in. But he is pretty cute, and I never thought I'd look at him that way. I've known him since he and his wife moved in across the street. The other 2 and I have only saw him as the cool neighbor, but now……………….

I hope he's safe. With mom and dad gone, I need him more than ever.

I mean we need him.

June 22
Tara's notes

Jess and Kyle both have a gun. That's okay, I don't really want one. They kind of scare me. But maybe he'll find another one and give it to me. I guess that'd be fine.

I was watching Jess with Collin, and she has got it bad for him. The way she looks at him and stuff is really gross. He's old, like 26 or something. Ew. I guess he's good looking, but I don't know. I'm going to ask Jess before Collin gets back what's going on with them. I hear some noise outside so I'm going to go check. I have to be sneaky so I don't get seen by whatever is going on. It sounds like some laughing and screaming.

It was 2 guys on the roof of a house not too far from us. They have a girl with them and they are doing things to her. Her screaming brought a bunch of deaders to them. They pointed then they threw her at the deaders' from the roof! Holy crap! They're tearing her apart. I think I'm going to barf!

June 22
Jess' notes

Tara told me about the 2 guys on the roof with the girl. She is really shaken up. Watching them do whatever to them and then throwing her off the roof! Kyle overheard us talking and he has his gun out! I tell him to put it away and cool it. We can't let those two jerks know where we are. If he tried to shoot them he's just going to bring the deaders to us. I ask him to just be calm, but be ready for anything.

I peek out the window and those guys are just sitting there. They look like they found the liquor store and are drinking. The zombies are underneath them trying like crazy to get them. I hope they do. Throwing pieces of roof at them is just making the zombies more desperate to get them. So, so, so, so, stupid. I grab the shotgun to be safe in case they see us. With Collin gone, I have to do everything I can to keep us safe. I wish he was here.

It's been a couple hours and it looks like there are twice as many deaders as was there before. The smell from those things is really awful. I see missing limbs, intestines hanging out, it's disgusting. The more noise they make, the more show up. And they're making a lot of noise. Those two are dumber than a bag of hammers.

Kyle was watching them, and he saw another guy on the ground running. The two idiots saw him and yelled for him to get up there with them! Amazingly, he made it up there with their help. Those 2 were actually being nice. Suddenly they pushed him off onto the deaders. He screamed as he fell and all of us heard it. I think he lasted 20 seconds. Kyle was really steaming, but he was also scared. He wanted to shoot them and I thought he was going to until I reminded him about being quiet. With Collin gone, we have to be extra careful.

I really hope he gets back soon. Please hurry, Collin!

June 23
Collin's notes

I almost made it to the city limits between Winlock and Napavine. I hope the kids are okay. Looks like Napavine is in the same shape as Winlock. There's the tavern everybody goes to. It looks like something is going on in there. I wished I had some binoculars. I'll get a little closer so I can see what might be happening. With any luck, maybe we can pool our resources with whoever is in there. It looks like there's a fire beside it; I'll move up and hope I don't get noticed by the group of deaders wandering about a hundred yards away.

Some activity going on. Two guys just dragged what looks like a kid outside. He's screaming! Are these guys stupid? That is going to get them all kinds of attention they don't need. Now what? One of the two just kicked the kid in the face too quiet him down. Now a women ran out with another guy following her trying to catch her! One of these jerks grabbed her and are holding her while she is still screaming! One of the guys pulls out a gun and shot her in the leg! There has to be a million zombies coming from everywhere. They're almost on top of them. The gun man shoots the kid in the leg, too. Then they bolt inside just as the deaders swarm the two people. Horrible! The screaming is just - bringing more and more. My God!

I don't know what the hell is going on here, but I'm going to find out!

The deaders cleared out after the "meal", leaving only a couple of stragglers. Machetes are awesome! The two go down without a problem. I'm going to listen in at the bar and find out what they are doing. I knew the guy that owned this place, and I can't believe he'd allow people to do this in here. Maybe this event changed him. For the worse. I know I'm not the same guy I was a month ago.

I figure out what's going on. The owner is walking around with half his intestines hanging out. I won't go into the smell but he looks like he's been dead for weeks. I can't stand to see him like this. I'm putting him down.

Three guys from out of town were trapped here when the outbreak happened. They made their way to the tavern and found four or five other people in there. Now the number is down by 2. And one of them was a kid! The remaining 3 besides the bastards are a senior citizen, a teenage boy who must be his grandson, and a 20 something women. Starting to get dark. I see a place right across the street that looks secure. I'm going to stay there and watch. Maybe I can do something about those three. Something needs to be done.

June 24

Those bastards did it to the other three! The old guy was thrown out and the kid right after! The one guy with the gun shot grandpa. The kid tried to fight back, but the son of a bitch shot him in the face! Then they tossed the girl down, and it looks like they…..well, her clothes are torn. There are about twenty deaders swarming the three. He didn't have the decency to shoot her. She tried to run, but she maybe got a few yards. That's it.

I can't let these three live. What would they do if they found the kids? I don't even want to think about it. I have to do this to keep them from getting to my kids. I mean the kids. God forgive me for what I'm about to do. I really hate what this is doing to me.

June 25

I've made a plan, then changed it. I was going to kick the door in and throw a bunch of fireworks, but I found 2 gallons of gasoline. I make sure the deaders are few and far between, but I'm still going to try to be quiet. I pour gas around the door frames, the lower windows and on the vehicles. I don't know if the cars belong to them, and I don't care. They are not getting away. I light fire crackers five feet from the door, and I make a gas line with the left over gas back to it. I light and run.

The bottom goes up like a tinder box. There is no way they can get out. And they prove me wrong. One of them comes flying out one of the windows on the first floor, but he's screaming. He looks about six feet tall, bald with a Duck Dynasty beard. Except the beards on fire. He rolls on the ground and is enveloped by deaders. He lasts about a minute. I see one of the others on the second floor. I think it's the gun man. The third one comes out the door completely covered in flames. He runs five feet and falls. No longer moving. I better move before I become a target for the deaders.

I run, hear a scream and a thud on the ground behind me. Turning, I see who it is. The gun man. He begs and pleads with me to help. I just stare at him. I told him I saw what he did to those people, and there was no way in hell I could let the three of them live. He cusses up a blue streak at me. "Who made you judge and jury? You stupid prick! I'll kill you!!" I remind him he doesn't have a gun. Plus, he has other problems. About twenty deaders are coming right at him. Too bad his leg broke when he fell. He might have lived to kill me. I turn my back and walk away as he is torn to pieces by the deaders.

I make it back to the safe house I was at and watch the tavern burn. It doesn't take as long as I thought. The building was pretty old I guess. I'm going to have to live with what I've just done. But I have to remind myself why I did it. For the kids. That is my justification. I will do anything to keep them safe.

I think I'm going to puke.

I just remembered something. The freeway isn't too far from here. I think I'll start working my way back in the morning. I can get the kids and maybe we can get out of here through Napavine. The high school is pretty close also. And maybe there are other survivors. I better get ready now so I can just grab my stuff and bolt.

June 24
Jess' notes

They saw me. The two guys on the roof heard the noise I made when I tripped. I hit so hard that it knocked some stuff off the outside of the house! I stood up and they saw me in the window. Then they pointed at the house and made some really gross gestures. One of them threw a liquor bottle so hard I heard it from here. The deaders went for the noise and the two guys jumped off the roof and started running toward us! I yelled for Tara to meet me at the door and we hammered more boards across the door as fast as we could. They got here and started pounding on the door, screaming what they wanted to do to me. Tara started to cry and I reached for my gun. Dang it! The guns are upstairs! We need to move!

Kyle is already in the room with the guns when we come in. He sees Tara and asks what was going on. I barricade the door and tell him to grab his nine millimeter. I pick up the shotgun praying I don't have to use it. I then hear wood splintering and the two guys coming in cussing and yelling what's going to happen to me. We huddle together, Kyle shaking as he points his gun toward the door, and me aiming the shotgun. Suddenly an axe makes a huge hole in the door and we scream. One of the guys sees Tara and tells his friend, "One for each of us! And a bonus! It's a little boy but who cares!" And he laughs. Kyle aims and fires, hitting the first guy right between the eyes. He falls down dead as the door opens. His friend picks up the axe and heads for Kyle. Kyle is shaking and crying, unable to point his gun. He lifts his axe to bring down on my brother, who is frozen with fear!

I fire the shot gun just as the axe is raised and the guy's head comes completely off. He falls backward out the door and lands with a thud on the floor. Tara is screaming and I think Kyle is in shock. I just killed a man. He was going to hurt my family, but I actually killed a man. Oh my God. Kyle killed someone too.

Collin where are you?

Kyle hasn't spoken for at least 3 hours. I hate that he lost his innocence in all this. All of us have. I thought losing mom and dad would be the worst, but I see I'm mistaken. Collin told us It isn't the dead we have to worry about it's the living. I can't believe everyone we come into contact with will be like those two, but I don't know. I need to make sure we're ready to leave when Collin gets back. After all that, I don't think we can stay here anymore.

Please, God, bring Collin back safely.

June 25
Tara's notes

After all the yelling and gun shots, a gajillion deaders have shown up outside the house. We fixed the holes the two butt-holes made, but they are still laying on the floor upstairs. The blood is super gross. Kyle is sitting in the other upstairs bedroom, just staring. I walked in to see if he was hungry, but he just shook his head. At least he smiled and said "No thank you." I can't imagine what he is thinking right now. I hope I never have to do what he and Jess did.

Speaking of Jess, all she's been doing is watching out the window for Collin. She really has the hots for him. He is nice and all, but he is so old! Man. Jess did go in and talk to Kyle and told him she was very proud of him. If he hadn't done what he did, we'd all be dead right now. She hugged him and he hugged her back, but he was crying. Jess told Kyle he did what he had to do, and it would be alright.

I hope Collin gets back soon. I want out of here.

June 26
Collin's notes

I'm about a half block from where the kids are, and the house is surrounded. Something bad must have happened. At least I've got a few fire crackers left and this machete. Crap. It looks like something got in! I never should have left the kids! I need to find the stupid fireworks.

Two strings left. Here goes the first one.
Good. The creeps are heading toward the noise, leaving me an easy enough path to get in the house. I see just a couple that should be no problem for Mr. Machete!

June 26
Jess' notes

I hear firecrackers! It must be Collin! The deaders have moved away; thank God none of them figured out how to walk up the stairs. I grabbed the gun and told Tara and Kyle to block the door best they can. I tell them to not open it except for me and Collin. I get outside and I see him! It is Collin and he is running superfast! I tell the other two to open the door so we can get in.

Collin's notes

I need to get Jess and the other two out of here as fast as possible. I may end up using our last bit of firecrackers to get us away, but it can't be helped. The deaders are distracted, and we have an opportunity. We better use it.
I get to the door but I was noticed. Inside I try to head up the stairs quickly, but not enough. A deader is following me up, hissing and whatever other noise he makes. Man, these things stink! I turn and he reaches for me. I introduce him to my machete by completely taking off his head and right shoulder. The body parts flop to the ground at just about the same time as the rest of him does.

Collin's notes

The kids make me feel like they haven't seen me for months! It is a nice welcome. Especially from Jess. Anyways, I get the kids moving. Ammo, guns, and a little food. I tell them we need to get out of here. I think I've found us a way to get to the freeway. I notice the two bodies, and decide I'll ask about it later. Ready to leave, we all see the deaders working their way back to us. I light the last string of crackers and throw them right at the head of one of them. He stops and stares at them as they go off. The rest follow suit and we are able to run without too much difficulty.
We get to a new place and hunker down for the night. Seems to be pretty secure, so we relax as much as we can. I don't see to many zombies walking around; at least they haven't noticed us so that's good. Kyle finds a couch and plops down on it. He's asleep in about four seconds. Tara gets on the floor next to him and passes out in less than a minute. I find some blankets and cover them, and then I make sure were as safe as possible. Jess finds a chair but stirs when she sees me walking around. She offers to help, but I tell her to take it easy. She is out like a light.
Jess is something. I need to remember how old she is, even though this place is making the three of them grow up too fast. She is very pretty girl, and she also has—No! Stop thinking like that you sick perv. I'm going to try and sleep too. We need to keep moving as soon as sun comes up.

June 27
Collin's notes

We are going to try and make a dash for Napavine. The kids want out of this and behind them as soon as possible. I don't blame them. My cousin Ryan lives up in Rochester, so if we can get out of here, that's where we are going. I think, if everything works in this "perfect world" we live in, I want to try and take custody these kids. I couldn't ask for a nicer bunch. They are fantastic.

I need to figure out a way to get a message to Ry. It's been a month, and I'm just wondering if this outbreak thing is just here? Or is the rest of the world affected?

Kids are ready. Time to go.

Jess' notes

Collin is awesome! We were running and suddenly we came upon like six or seven deaders. Collin pulled out his machete and just went to town! One deader came at Collin and he cut him from shoulder to hip. He got between deaders and us and just cut them to pieces! Tara threw up when she saw that. It didn't help when Collin hacked the rest while we ran. I think it was the smell from the dead people. It is really nasty. When Collin was chopping, I thought Kyle's eyes were going to pop out of their sockets.

It was just super-sexy watching him. Oh my God!

Tara's notes

Jess is being really retarded. She is so ga ga over Collin she's being stupid. Although, what he did was pretty cool, even though it made me throw up. The deaders stink! I don't think anyone else could take care of us as well as Collin has. I hope we get to see him when all this is done.

June 29
Collin's notes

We've been lucky so far. We're almost to the tavern, and it is actually still smoldering. We come up to it and Jess grabs my hand. I don't pull away. In fact, I hold it tighter and she gives me a smile that could melt the sun! I finally tell the kids what happened here and what I did. I talk about what the three guys were doing and why I felt it necessary to stop it. There was no way on Earth that I was going to allow these maniacs the chance to find us; then "take care of us" the way they did the others. Kyle surprises me by grabbing my other hand and saying, "You did what you had to so we'd be safe. It's okay." Tara also hugs me and shakes her head yes. Jess just smiles. I stop and hug the three of them, and I never want to let them go!

I tell them to break it up and cool it while chuckling. They all do the same and it feels good to find a little humor in this hell-hole. The deaders are few and far between, which is good. We head to the place not far from where I stayed the first time I was in this area. It's a house with like four bedrooms, two baths and what looks like a rec room. Not to mention it seems pretty secure.

I'm feeling like we might make it, but I don't want to get any of our hopes up.

June 30
Collin's notes

Today, around daybreak, I see a woman walking around not far from us. About 30 yards away, carrying some kind of satchel. She was not using her brain at all because she kept yelling for her husband, a kid, or something. I don't see many deaders around; they are about three to four blocks away, but they won't be for long. Not if she keeps yelling like that. I'm going to go get her. Probably won't make the kids too happy, but she doesn't look like she's too dangerous. I better get moving.

I was right. The kids aren't happy one bit. Jess mentioned that how do we know we can trust her? What if she spazzes out and tries to kill us in our sleep? And lots of other questions. The other two kids agree. I let them know that she is older. Even than me. Plus, we have weapons. We all decide to stay in the same room tonight while she is here; so they feel safer.

I talk to her and find out her name is Carla. She is in her early 50s and looking for her husband. It seems he collapsed at home, and his heart stopped. She didn't know what to do with him. I thinking she was in such a state of shock that she lost it. Carla told me she went to her room and cried herself to sleep. After a few hours, she awoke to find him gone! I did try to explain what was going on, but she is completely adamant about finding him. I invite her to walk with us to Napavine, and she agrees to go with us until she finds her husband. I don't know what she thinks is going to happen when she finds him. I pretty sure she is going to be in for a terrible surprise.

July 1
Collin's notes

Heading out the door, and the streets seem pretty empty. There are a few straggling deaders about three blocks away. As long as we stay at a steady, descent pace, we should be able to keep the blocks distant from them. They can be persistent, but they certainly don't move fast. I think we'll still stop at a house in a couple hours just to get off the street for a while. No use taking unnecessary chances.

Carla is not helping the situation at all. Every so often she yells for her husband; thinking he is going to answer. She got an answer alright. A deader came out between a couple houses and went right for her. If Tara hadn't hollered I wouldn't have been able to get out the machete in time. Everyone is shaken up, but okay. If this happens again, we're cutting her loose.

We got a little farther and saw a place to hang out for the night. Carla lagged behind us for about half a block which was good. She started yelling again, and I finally told her she was putting all of us in danger. If she wants to keep doing that she is on her own.

She doesn't care. We got to a house and got in before anything happened. Carla followed us in and I got the door shut up nicely before the deaders got to us. All her yelling drew about fifty deaders to where we're at. I'm telling the kids. Tomorrow we let her go.

It was night time when I found Carla outside with a flash light shining it around. Doesn't she know the zombies will come to the light, especially if they see it moving? I know she is grieving, but she is going to get herself and the rest of us killed! Before I can do anything, she spots her husband and runs to him. I try to get to her, but I'm too late. She wraps her arms around him, and holds him tight. I guess he didn't know what was going on. He looked surprised, but it quickly went away as he bit her ear off. All I could do was watch as she screamed. Her husband bit into her again and she went down on the ground. Soon there were about eight deaders all over her and that was it. I turned and went back into the house and shut the door. The kids asked what the screaming was, and I told them Carla found her husband. I didn't have to say anymore. Even Kyle understood.

I'm just glad the screaming finally stopped.

July 3
Collin's notes

      Got pretty busy yesterday so I was unable to record. Out looking for food, and I came across some canned meet, carrots and even a propane stove with fuel. Took me two trips to get everything. To avoid the deaders walking around it took me six hours to get everything back to our little "safe house". I noticed that there are quite a few more of the dead walking around than before. They look new. Like recently deceased new. Or maybe a better phrase would be "dead-ized". The dozen or so I saw were covered in blood, and the ones I got close enough too had chunks of their necks missing. Great. Vampire zombies. It just keeps getting better and better.
      I thought I saw an army soldier recently deceased. Maybe the military finally made it down here, or he just wandered to the area. If that's the case, the whole state might be affected. If not the whole country. I don't know what we're going to do when and if we get out of here.
      We made pretty good time getting here. We're almost to Napavine High School, which is not too far from the freeway. I think that would be the best place for now. It's big enough that even if some deaders got in, we shouldn't have trouble avoiding them. Plus, it's possibly only a few hours from here, and not a few days. I get with the kids and will make a plan to leave tomorrow.

July 4
Collin's notes

Happy fricking fireworks day. We made it a total of two blocks before we were almost caught by a huge freaking horde of deaders. There has got to be at least a thousand between where were at and the high school. Tara surprised me when I saw her climb up on the roof out of one of the windows in this two story house we ducked into. I was a little worried until I joined her. It wasn't so bad. We saw the road to the high school which is almost a straight shot from where we are at. Except that between us and the school is like fifty deaders. They aren't just in an area we could go around, they are spread out so much we can't avoid them. No matter what we try to do. It is kind of weird. Where the hell did they all come from?

July 5
Tara's notes

Collin is thinking about going out and trying to find another way to the high school. I don't want him to go, and Jess is totally freaking out. He did tell us we are going to have a food and water problem eventually, and we need to do something soon. He just wants to go across the street to a house, but there are like a million deaders out there and I don't think he'll make it. Even if the house is only like a hundred feet away. The stinky dead guys smell worse than the dump! I remember going with dad and thinking it was cool. I miss him and mom.

Now Kyle thinks he wants to go with Collin! Why do boys always want to do stuff that makes them think they look tough? Boys are so stupid.

July 5
Jess' notes

Sometimes I just want to kill Collin. He wants to just go across the street to look for food, but the whole neighborhood is crowded with zombies! To make matters worse, Kyle wants to go with him! Ugh!!! I don't want Collin to die just because we're hungry. Kyle, too. I honestly cannot help how I feel about Collin. I don't care how much older he is. Is it because of what's going on? Because he has kept us safe? Doesn't matter. I can't help feeling this way.

Kyle is completely different than when all this started. Just 4 months ago he had to still sleep with the lights on in his room, and now he's actually shooting people to keep us alive. Well, one person anyways. I hate that his innocence is gone. I hate the fact Tara and I have done things I would never have dreamed of six months ago.

Before this is over, I'm going to tell Collin how I feel about him.

July 6
Collin's notes

We have a few fireworks left. I found an M-80, and outside next to an SUV is a propane tank. I wonder what genius thought of that? This is on the opposite of the house we're in from the street. My idea is to throw the M-80 at the propane tank and pray that it explodes. Hopefully the noise will draw the deaders to it and we can bolt across the street to the other houses. There is a small problem.

Both the tank and SUV are fairly close to the house, and I don't know what kind of reaction that will have. Will it set off the vehicle too? I guess I better meet with the family. Let them know what I'm planning. Huh. I always wanted to say that, but with the wife.

I'm sure glad Jess is here.

We are going to go through with this tomorrow. It seems pretty risky, but I'm out of ideas. The kids need food, and we're getting low. First thing in the morning we are gone out of here.

July 7
Collin's notes

       I just threw out the last string of firecrackers to get the deaders attention. Jess yelled that it was working. I see about ten coming around the side of the house. I light the M-80 and run for the door. It works. We haul ass outside as we hear the 80 go off. Then the propane tank followed by the SUV. The explosion engulfs the house and must have hit a gas mane or something. The house explodes and sends all four of us flying. I'm the first up and I quickly get the other three. It's raining pieces of bodies all over the place as we try to get as far away as we can. A deader lands right by Kyle, with one third of a body. The third has a head, and arm and part of a torso. It has just of enough "life" to grab Kyle's leg and make him trip. He screams help, and before I can get to him, Jess is next to him stomping the head of the deader flat! She picks up Kyle and catches up with Tara and I and we book.

       As fast as we were moving, it still was not quick enough. Three deaders almost caught up with us. I run back and machete the hell out of them and make sure I give us plenty of breathing space. We make it to a house a little bit closer to the high school. That's the good news. The bad news is the explosion drew more deaders to the scene, and just about doubled them. We may not have as far to go, but it is going to be twice as hard to get there.

July 7
Tara's notes

When we got in this house, Jess went and hugged Kyle. He was still freaked out by the deader grabbing him. I'm just glad he is okay. Collin is outside trying to get the "sit-rep" of the area. That's what he says he is doing. I don't understand what it means. He is trying to find the quickest route to the high school. A deader grabbed at him, and pulled out his machete and cut his hands off. Then he turned and took the head off right below the collar bone! It was kind of gross, but Collin is AWESOME!

I told Jess and Kyle what he did, and it was like I told her a movie star wanted to be her boyfriend. She is so weird.

Jess' notes

Collin is walking around just outside while Tara and Kyle watch. It looks like we are about eight to ten blocks from the high school. Which is maybe a ten-minute walk, but considering the town is overrun with zombies, it is probably a two-day walk. It's like walking through an African wild life preserve, and the lions haven't been fed for a week. And they'll eat anything.

A deader grabbed Collin by the arm and almost bit him! He got free and turned with his machete and cut his head in half. He kicked it as it fell and he ran across the street. He waved to us and went in.

He's coming back. It is like he was gone for hours, but I know it's only been a few minutes. Now I know I got it really bad for him.

Collin's notes

We are going to leave this house for the one across the street. It isn't as big, but it feels a lot safer than where we are at. I get them up and ready. Jess has the shotgun, Kyle the pistol, and Tara is carrying the backpack of supplies we have left. Which is nothing. I told them to sprint and I will be right behind them. Both are smart enough to only use the guns in a dire emergency. Like there isn't one. We're ready.

Tara tripped! She got banged up pretty good, but she is still mobile. She dropped the backpack, but I tell her to forget it and move! Three deaders are almost on her before she can get two feet. I kick one into a "girl" deader and they both go down. The third one lunges at me, but I cut his head off at the shoulder. While he falls I stab the girl in the head as I stomp the last one's head. Flat. We get into the other place and finally relax as much as we can.

I secure the door and head over to check on Tara. Her arm is pretty banged up, but she is going to be fine. I think we'll stay at least a day until Tara feels good enough. I found plenty of food in here, so we could hold out a couple days. I suppose we'll wait and see.

July 8

There is a house that is actually pretty close to us. I decide to let Kyle come with me. Jess isn't very happy about it, and I understand. He's been wanting to go on a run with me for a while, and I figure the house is close enough that we should be safe. I promise nothing will happen to him, and the first sign of trouble we'll come right back. She gives me a smile that could thaw Antarctica, and kisses me on the cheek. I realize the situation is making the kids grow up fast. Maybe certain feelings are happening because of what we're dealing with, but she is like ten years younger than me! Plus, my wife just died! I should not be even thinking like this. If she were twenty and I was thirty, that's different. Not fifteen and 25. That is not cool. Still, she does have a pretty nice-

NO! NO! NO! NO! NO! NO! NO! NO! NO! NO! Stop thinking that!

Kyle and I are back from a neighboring house, and I realize we are closer to Napavine High School than I first thought. Tara is recovering from her fall even though she is still a little sore. I'm thinking we need to head to the school tomorrow and start making a serious plan to get the hell out of here. I've had it with the zombies, the running, and danger from the live people who are even worse than the deaders. There really aren't as many deaders around right now. Which I think is odd, but I don't dwell on it.

Then Kyle and I hear something that sounds like a chainsaw! I send him back to the house. I want to check it out. Good thing it's within a half a block, and he sprints as fast as he can. I take a discretionary walk to the noise and see the most incredible thing I've seen since all this started. A guy, about 6 foot 9 in a t-shirt, suspenders, and I think combat boots. I then realize they are logging boots. I should try to remember where I am. The chainsaw he's holding is idling when three deaders come at him. It roars as he cuts two of the three in half at the waist and they flop on the ground still trying to grab him. The third lunges and the logger grabs him by the head and slams him so hard on the ground it explodes into a million pieces! The saw revs again as he uses it to pulp the heads of the two half deaders.

He looks around as if expecting more trouble. Seeing none, he puts the chainsaw over his shoulder and walks toward the high school. A couple feet away, the mountain of a man picks up what looks like a double bladed axe and continues on.

If we meet him, I'm going to try really hard to stay on his good side.

July 10

We decide to make a try for the high school. It's a straight shot if we sprint. There are a few deaders between us that could be a problem, but not enough we shouldn't be able to out maneuver. Jess has the shotgun, Kyle the pistol and Tara a backpack. We head out when all of us hear the chainsaw revving up. I look and see the logger swinging it and taking out the dead walkers left and right, but there are too many. I have to help him.

Jess' notes

The biggest man I've ever seen is swinging a chainsaw and cutting down deaders like a weed whacker on tall grass. We stop and look, then Collin decides to go help him! He tells us to keep running but we don't. Kyle and Tara start screaming as a deader comes at us. I shoot his hand off and the three of us run!

Body parts fly everywhere as Collin and the giant are cutting them down with the saw and machete. They were back to back as Collin saw an opening to catch up with us. They both come running and we get to the school. Collin and the big logger covered in blood and guts. The logger stands by Collin and pats him on the back. Collin almost falls and both laugh. The big guy says he'll help us out. He looks at the three of us and gives us the "sup" nod. We all smile back and giggle little. We all walk into the school.

After watching Collin go at those zombies like he did, I want him so bad right now it hurts!

July 13
Collin's notes

Been a couple days. We're settled in and even got our own room. It's a classroom, but beggars can't be choosers. There is food, water, showers and even laundry machines to wash our clothes. There's also a lot more people here than I thought would be. Maybe forty or fifty.

There's two guys here that have been watching Jess and Tara a little too closely for my tastes. Kyle walked by them and overheard make some comments about his sisters that really pissed him off. I better hold on to the pistol until he cools down. These guys are in their late teens, early twenties as far as I can tell. But this event has aged everybody, so who knows their age. I'm going to watch them close. They'll learn a hard lesson if they touch Jess!

And Tara too.

When we got here we met Reverend Hal Jones. He is the head guy at the non-denominational Church in town. I'm not much of a church guy, but Tara was asking him all kinds of questions. One she asked that I'll never forget was why God let this happen. He said, "God didn't do this. It was man trying to play God, and this is the result of their folly." Then they got into some other topics and I decided to go check on Kyle. He was talking to the logger who said we could just call him Forester. Kind of funny in a way. A logger named Forester. Well, Forester it is.

Those two guys tried to corner Jess. I got over to them in time and told them to back off! They were just about to try something when Forester came up behind me with his double sided axe. They proved to be smarter than they looked and left. They both smelled like they hadn't bathed since all this started. Their clothes were ragged and dirty like they'd slept in a mud puddle for two months. Teeth were gone too, so I'm thinking they were meth heads.

I'll be taking extra precautions tonight, with those two around. Probably won't sleep. I Hope Forester isn't too far away.

July 14
Tara's notes

        The two gross guys came to our room on the second floor! They must have followed us. One of them hit Collin so hard I think he is knocked out! The other one pinned Jess against the wall. Kyle tried to help but there was no way he could have done anything. Every time Collin tried to get up the one who was watching us kicked him down and laughed! He got the shot gun from me before I could do anything. Jess is crying, begging for the guy to stop touching her. He slaps her and laughs! I don't know what to do-Forester just came in! He has his axe and he swings it and cuts the guy with the gun arm off. I grab it and shoot. The guy flies back into a chalk board, splattering all over the place. I puke.

        The other guy turns and starts screaming he'll hurt Jess! Jess punches him in the privates and runs over to us. The guy falls down clutching himself as Forester grabs him by the throat and lifts him with one hand! We can hear him having a hard time breathing as forester walks him to the window. He doesn't even open it as he throws him through it! I don't watch him fall, but I hear him screaming all the way to the ground. Forester picks up the dead guy and throws him out the same window. The screaming woke Collin up. He was still pretty dizzy, and Forester picked him up like a baby and started to carry him to the door. He told us to follow him down to the gym. As we left, the one live guy was still screaming as we could hear the deaders ripping him to shreds.

        Collin was feeling a little better but he said his head hurt. Pastor Hal is also a doctor. He said he left that, but still has his license, to answer the call to be a minister. He is pretty cool. He told us that Collin has a slight concussion, but he should be fine. Forester tells him about the attack by the two meth heads, but Pastor Hal doesn't ask about what happened to them.

        I'm sure glad Forester decided to be our friend. Kyle likes him, and Forester always stops and talks with him. We find another place to rest for the night, and Forester actually camps right outside our door. Jess, of course, goes over and lays down right next to Collin so she can "help" him if he needs it. Yeah, right. She is so weird. Everyone is asleep but me, but I think I'll try to now. Tomorrow, I think we are going to make a plan to get a move on. I really want to get out of here, but I want to stay with Collin from now on. I think the others do too! Especially Jess.

July 15
Collin's notes

    I feel a lot better today. My head doesn't hurt as bad as yesterday, but it still is throbbing. I look around for the kids; nowhere to be found. I find them in the gym talking to Hal, and I approach. Hal wants to know how I am, and I tell him. He lets me know that I should be fine in another day or two, but I need to take it easy. I ask where Forester is because I want to thank him. If it wasn't for him, well, I really don't want to think about it.

    Hal said that he went out to do some recon. Some people came in while I was out cold and said that the military finally showed up. But it wasn't good. They said they weren't sure, but it looked like the soldiers were killing survivors! I look confused and Forester comes running in. "We need to get out of here now!" he yells. The soldiers are killing everyone they come into contact with that isn't a zombie. Including kids! We don't ask questions as we collect our belongings and try to bolt. Forester, the kids and I are together. Hal doesn't come with us. He is going to try and get as many of the people out as he can. I hope he makes it.

    We round a corner on the ground floor as three soldiers appear right in front of us. They take aim. Before they can shoot, Forester hurls his double bladed axe at one of them. Splitting his chest completely open. The other two don't get a shot off before Forester gets to them, his chainsaw blaring. He stabs it into the soldier on the right and revs it up. With his other hand he smacks the other one. He goes down with a thump, but not before he flew ten feet! Forester turns back from his handy work and picks up the other soldier and slams him against the wall! It actually cracked! I'm sure glad he's our friend!

    "TALK!" Forester shouts. We all hear gunfire and start to get really nervous. The soldier, in tears, tells us what's going on. Apparently, the military is here on a mission called "Operation Purge". They were ordered by the commanding officer of Fort Lewis to not take chances and shoot anything that moves in these two towns. This particular group's job was to try and contain this outbreak, but they failed. It has officially covered the entire state of Washington as far as he knows. This is just a rumor he said he heard, but the evidence is there. The big brass said it's contained, but they are getting communications from other bases in the state of the break out of walking dead. This is too much.

    The military is supposed to work its way back to the building in Winlock with the swastikas on the top. I have never understood why those were up there. Probably some kind of KKK thing. I guess there is a lab or something in the building. I just don't know how it got in there without anyone finding out. Forester looks at me and says, "I think I know. As soon as we put some distance between us and this place, I'll fill you in."

    Forester thanks the soldier by hitting him again and knocking him out. We take their weapons and head out. We're going back to Winlock.

    More gunfire now. We either move or join the rest of the people in the school.

July 16
Jess' notes

Collin is still not perfect, but he is better. I guess the hit on the head really hurt him. Forester said he'd stay with us until we got to Winlock. I think maybe he is looking for someone too. I don't know. He grabs his axe and says he's going to go find some food. I'm glad we met him. He is super cool!

This house we're in isn't too far from the high school, but it is in a spot where I think we'll be safe from the soldiers and the occasional deader. Collin is going to try to get on the roof and see if he can see anything. I think he's worried about Reverend Hal. I know Hal went back to help people get away from the military. I just don't understand why they were killing us. Something about a purge? I thought we finally got some help; instead they were shooting everyone in sight! That might mean that Hal is-no. I'm not going to think that. The best part is Collin is up moving around, Kyle and Tara are safe, and we have a new friend who is like The Incredible Hulk with a chainsaw. I think we're going to be okay.
I hope so anyways.

Collin's notes

Forester saved our collective asses. Jess and the kids are fine, I'm doing a lot better, and we've got a friend I wish I had in high school. Jess is watching me like a hawk. I'm still not 100%. Those two guys beat the crap out of me, and she has been by my side every minute since. I don't what I'd do without her.
Or the other two kids.

Two thirds of the soldiers that attacked the school are either dead, deaders, or they've bugged out. I can see soldiers lumbering around; missing arms, covered in blood, and even chewing on what looks like other people's body parts. I will never get used to that no matter how many times I see it. All the shooting that happened just drew more deaders to the school, and then they overwhelmed the soldiers. They got what they deserved the pricks. A purge team? What is that? And why here? Is everywhere else affected? Something isn't making sense. I hope Forester gets back soon. He said he saw something one night, and I wonder if that has anything to do with what's going on.
I need to look for a working radio. Maybe someone is broadcasting and we can get some info. I probably should've thought of this a little sooner than now. Oh well. Live and learn. I see Forester is back with some canned goods. I think I'll ask him what he knows. I'm pretty sure he doesn't want the kids to hear what he has to say.
That kind of bugs me. A little.

July 17
Collin's notes

Everyone is pretty well rested, and full of food. Thanks to Forester. I ask the kids to wait in the other room while Forester and I talk. I let them know it isn't a big deal, but he wants to talk about something he saw. I'm not sure that they need to hear it. Yet. We actually walk outside instead and it is a pretty nice night. We sit on the porch; not seeing any deaders, and he tells me what he saw.

"Before all this started," he says, "I saw something really weird downtown." I still laugh when I hear that. "Downtown Winlock." If people saw the size of this community, they'd think we were in a ghost town that doesn't know it is a ghost town. That is how small it is. Forester continues. "The building with the swastikas on the top of it is where it all began. I get up about two a.m. every morning to get to work. As I was heading to my rig, I see a bunch of lights at the building, and a bunch of guys walking around the outside of it. All were holding what looked like automatic weapons. Well, since I'm a little smarter than I look," I laugh a little. He stops and giggles, "I duck between houses behind some bushes, but I can still see everything. None of the guys looked like soldiers, but they had military jeeps and stuff. There was a big truck, and they were unloading some scientific equipment. At least that what it looked like. They didn't see me; I guess they didn't have any night-vision goggles, otherwise I'd be dead. They shot a guy who was staggering around drunk. I didn't recognize him, but I thought it was kind of weird."

He stops talking and decides to stand and walk toward the street. What he says makes me think. Is this a military operation? I watch Forester, and he looks like he is shaking. Maybe even sobbing. He is looking at a picture of some kind. I catch a glimpse of it and it looks like a woman and young girl. Family? Whoever it is, he isn't happy about it. I take the better part of valor and get out of his way. He is extremely pissed off. We both head in the house for the night and he grabs both his chainsaw and axe. With one hand. Wow. He sits and sharpens the axe, and I think I wouldn't want to be the person who made this giant of a man this upset. I almost feel bad about the guys in the building we're going to. But if they are responsible for what happened here, I'm going to help Forester put them down.

I decide not to tell the kids and Jess about what Forester told me. If they think someone in our own country could do this to the people that live here, they are going to want to move to Canada. Why would anyone want to make something that hurts the land they live? Including the population? Isn't that treason? If that is true, my opinion of the government just got lower. And I thought they were a bunch of jack-asses before.

July 16

        I hope Tara doesn't mind me using her note book. She dropped or forgot it when the military showed up at the school. I believe it prudent to continue this narrative in case someone finds this to stop it from happening again. My name is Hal Jones, pastor at the non-denominational church here in Napavine. I was fortunate to get out of the school. I guess God is going to use me in this new world man has created. Meeting Collin and the children was good. A very nice bunch. Although, it seemed something inappropriate was happening between Collin and the older girl Jess. I believe that is her name. I may have a talk with him, providing he is still alive, and I find them the Lord willing.

        After the military attack, and subsequent overrunning of the school by the dead walkers, I am going to do my best to find Forester and the others. He mentioned that they wanted to head back to Winlock, so I guess that is where I'm going. I pray God leads me to them, and that he delivers us from this disaster. The mistake the soldiers made when the dead things attacked was shooting them in the chest. Or even shooting them at all. The noise drew more and more of the creatures to us, and they were overcome. Shooting them in the torso just slowed them down, and they kept coming at the soldiers. Uh oh, I can hear one shuffling close by. I better take cover.

        It wasn't a zombie. It was PFC Kimberson. He's missing his left arm at the bicep. As a doctor I quickly try to help him, but realize that there is no hope. An artery his shooting blood like a squirt gun. He collapses, and I see the bite marks on his arm. He explains "Operation Purge" and his part in it. I still forgive him, though I can't figure out why. The next thing planned for this "operation" is to bomb both towns. But he doesn't think that will happen considering the state of everything from Fort Lewis to here. He then asks me for a favor.

        He wants me to kill him. He has no hope for survival anyways, and Pvt. Kimberson doesn't want to turn into one of the dead things. I don't think I can do that. My job is to help save souls, not take lives. Instead, I hand him his pistol, and he points it at his head. Before he can pull the trigger, he hands me his M16 and extra ammo, thanking me. I choose not to watch and walk away. I hear him crying then a shot. Since I know it will draw more of the zombies, I run.

        I say a prayer for him hoping he is forgiven. I then pray I catch up with the others. We need to find a way out of here as soon as possible.

July 17
Hal's notes

    I come across a sight I'll take to my grave. It is the most horrible thing I've ever seen. I cannot understand what makes people do the things they do in a disaster. Taking advantage of others and doing things that I would never dream of. Heavenly Father, please don't let me get to the point where to survive I have to commit atrocities like I witnessed.

    Three women, four men are circling a teen girl and they look like they are chanting or praying. The girl is in tears and pleading with them to let her go. She even promises to anything they ask and begins to unbutton her shirt. Three of the men grab her and tie her to a tree. Soon the three are kneeling in front of the other man with the women. The standing man lifts a butcher's cleaver and walks to the girl. She screams. The other six people prostrate themselves like the man with the knife is a god! Sickening! The knife wielding man turns to the girl, and gently kisses her forehead. He thrusts the knife into her and she screams even louder. Blood is pouring out of her as the remainder of the group rises and rushes the tree. All pull out knives and begin slashing her flesh and eating it! Enough! I'm ending this before their attention is turned to other survivors. God, forgive me for what I'm going to do.

    Fortunately for me, I'm saved the trouble. A huge group of undead come from nowhere and attacks the seven. Try as they might, they are unable to do anything as the people are torn to shreds. The girl's screams must have drawn them here. I feel guilty for what I'm feeling right now. I feel pleased that this group of individuals won't be able to hurt anyone else. I think the guilt comes from what I was going to do to stop them. This environment is changing me. I don't believe in Karma. The true definition of it has been replaced by a "westernized" version of it. I do, however, believe you reap what you sow. The seven psychopathic people are living proof, I mean proof, of that.

    I better get a move on to Winlock. The dead might decide I'm an after dinner snack.

July 19
Hal's notes

I haven't had any problems for some time. I've been able to avoid the dead walkers, and actually get to some fairly safe places. I hope Tara doesn't mind me adding to her notebook. I pray that they are all safe, and that I'll find them.

I come across my neighbor Aaron. As happy as I am to see him; he seems angry at me. He starts yelling about how God could do this, then he actually starts to accuse me of being part of this. He says because I "speak" for God. He pushes me. I raise the M16 and he quickly calms himself. He must not have seen it. I try to explain that God is not responsible for this. He wants all of us to return to him. He would never create something like this to hurt his children. I believe, I tell Aaron, that this is a man-made virus. Man, in his quest to create, decided that he is smarter than God, and that we no longer need Him. So, he creates something to put life into the dead, setting himself up to be god. Every time a person tries to play god, it backfires with disastrous results. Hence our current situation. He tells my I'm a crazy bastard and walks away. I think this is the last time I'll ever see him.

But it's true. Man kills God, tries to be God, and turns into the devil. Man could never kill God, but the evil that man does in the name of science isn't science. I pray for Aaron and continue on. I hope he is safe and finds the truth.

July 21
Hal's notes

Took me two days to finally get to Winlock. I see that some of the recently turned are military. The only good thing about them being in the condition they're in is that they can't use their weapons anymore. I see a soldier come out from behind a house trying to run. He slips and falls and is smothered by deaders. That is what Tara and the rest call them. It is terrible. All he can do is scream, and that just brings more to rip him apart. His death enables me to move unmolested by the zombies. I pray for him and his sacrifice, even though he didn't know it. I see the building from where I'm at, and proceed to get to it.

Then I hear more screaming! It seems to be coming from the area of the building. Then there is gun fire! Multiple shots! I get as close as I can, but can't do much more. The shots drew a ton of deaders to the building. I try to hope for the best, but I'm pretty sure I'm not going to like what I find.

July 18
Collin's notes

    Forester got us to the building. I still don't understand the swastikas, but I suppose it doesn't really matter anymore. The deader population has thinned out since we've been here. Still a few here and there, but nothing I couldn't handle. Forester could probably take them out in his sleep. He and I were talking on the way here, and it turns out he has a degree in mechanical engineering. I never would have guessed. After the economy crashed; he lost his job came back here and was lucky to get on with a logging company. He logged a little in high school and before he went to college. I never met him in town before let alone seen him around. But, he loved what he was doing and said he never should've left. He is a hunter, fisherman and any other outdoor thing. I feel bad for him. Well, for all of us. But I do not want to be the person on the other end of this outbreak; if that person started it.

    We get in, but we weren't really noticed by anything. Forester opened a door, but he wasn't gentle. Or quiet. As we enter we see a bunch of bio-hazard containers. A closer check on them shows them all full! Other containers are labeled and filled with viruses! Bubonic Plague, Avain Flu, Rabies! Some are labeled with names I can't even pronounce! What the hell is going on here? All of us head up a flight of stairs past rooms filled with a bunch of equipment. Microscopes, incubators, high end super computers. I'm a high school English teacher and I don't have a clue on what any of this stuff is. All the vials, and cages? What the-? We make it to the top and find another lab, and something else. A guy in a lab coat is sitting on the floor crying.

    I think we just found the reason for the deader outbreak.

Collin's notes

I had to pull Jess off the scientist guy before she killed him! I thought for sure it would be Forester I'd have to try and stop. If he hadn't been there, I don't think I could've stopped her. I'd never seen anyone just lose it that quick before. She was hitting, kicking, and yelling about her parents. Tara and Kyle are trying to get her to calm down, but it isn't really working. I hold her back as Forester walks over to the scientist. He stands up, and Jess really kicked the crap out of him! He is really bleeding out of his nose, cuts on his face, and his lab coat is even ripped. Now I have to worry about not pissing Jess off.

He begins to tell us his story. He was contacted by a general after he was fired from the CDC. His specialty is in pathology and biology. Kyle asks what pathology is, and the scientist says it is the study of diseases. The general knew about his work, and wanted him to help provide a biological weapon to use against the enemies of our country. Not being a stupid man, he informed the general of the ban and the illegal production of such weapons. The scientist said that it is approved by the president and congress, and it would be a covert operation. They choose Winlock because of its accessibility to Interstate five, and short distance from Joint Base Lewis/Mchord. The general felt that it was an out of the way little town that no one would notice. Well, he was completely wrong. The scientist thinks that one of test subjects he injected with the virus escaped, and it went south from there.

Forester grabs him by the throat with one hand and lifts him off the ground. He slams him against the wall and raises his other hand to smash his face in. The scientist, barely audible, says that there is a vaccine the general doesn't know about. With both hands, Forester throws him through beakers, vials, and other equipment and he lands with a thud on the opposite side of a counter. I walk up to him and kneel, pointing the gun I'm carrying at his head. I ask him, "Give me one good reason why I shouldn't blow your damn head off? Why would you do this to people in our own country? Or anywhere? You don't deserve to live, you stupid bastard!" Before I can shoot, he tells me that we can get the vaccine and where it is. The problem, he broke up the necessary ingredients to make it and sent them to five completely different parts of the state. He sent them to former colleagues, college classmates, and his brother whom he hasn't spoken to in ten years.

I stand him up. I tell him to write down where they are exactly, the names of the people who have them, and directions. He does, and I hand the directions to Forester for safe keeping. He doesn't give addresses, but he does give coordinates and a GPS.

We look at each other, and decide we should be safe for a while. The scientist says that he has enough food to last for probably six months, and enough room for all of us to stay. Plus, there are showers for all of us. One thing has kind of been bothering me. There is still power to parts of the Town. Why? The scientist doesn't have an answer. I guess the infrastructure hasn't broken down yet. At least too much. Will wonders never cease?

July 21
Collin's notes

We've been here a few days, and everyone has freshened up. They all seem to feel much better. They've eaten, showered and even found a change of clothes. The kids are laughing, which is nice. Forester, however, hasn't done anything. He is staring daggers at the professor. I ask him why the power is still on in parts of the town. He doesn't have an answer, but they added a solar powered generator on the roof. So this place will never have a problem. Theoretically. The scientist sets up games for the kids on some of the computer; he wanted to talk to Forester and myself for some reason. We head to a part where we are out of ear shot of the kids and he tells us.

Somehow, the General found out about the vaccine. One of the soldiers got word to him that a team was coming to the building. That was part of the reason for the purge team. The other was to make sure that the virus didn't spread. They failed. He shows us pictures from across the state. There is an air force base in Spokane that was completely wiped out. He patched into a live feed on the base showing a motor pool. It is completely overrun by deaders. Forester gets even angrier than before, and he makes a suggestion. He wants to head out and find everything we need to get the vaccine. I ask about the kids, and he say that they will be safer with the two of us than with this prick. I agree.

Before we can tell the kids, we hear gun shots and one of the kid's scream. It sounds like Jess! We head out. What we see freezes my blood. Two soldiers, with pistols pointing them at the girls. On the ground, I only see Kyle's feet, and he isn't moving. My worst fears are confirmed.

And neither one of us has any of our weapons.

Hal's notes

I approach the building worrying about what I'll find, but I'm stopped by four soldiers. One of them is a colonel, a corporal, a private and someone they are calling chief. If I remember my military ranks, he is a chief warrant officer. All are pointing the weapons at me, and being a fairly smart man, I put down my M16. I tell them who I am and what I'm doing here. They are here for almost the same reason. The colonel asks about the gun, and I tell him of PFC Kimberson. They must have decided I wasn't a threat and allow me to pick up my weapon and join them. The man they call Chief looks at me, and reassures me that we'll get the kids and the other two out of here.

Suddenly from the building, we hear more gun shots and what sounds like a young persons' scream. I believe it is a girl- God no! Please don't let me find what I'm afraid is in there.

The building is surrounded by too many of the dead walkers. The corporal and private offer to create a diversion and draw as many away as possible. The chief puts his hand on the private and says he'll say a prayer for both. The colonel turns and salutes both, telling them it was an honor to serve with them. Both respond with a salute, but neither have any intention of not coming back. Smiling, they agree to meet at their transport and then they depart, guns blazing. The dead follow, and prove to be very slow. We head into the building, and I'm worried about what we'll find.

We get to the top and my worst fears are realized.

Hal's notes

        The Colonel and the Chief aim their guns at the two soldiers. Forester looks like he wants to rip both of the two to pieces. One of the two soldiers who is a lieutenant, turns suddenly to shoot and the Colonel fires. Hits him right in the face. The other soldier, it turns out is a major, starts yelling at us that we have no clue what is going on. Forester, sees an opportunity and practically flies and takes the major down! Pinning the major he starts to pound on his face. Repeatedly! The Col. Orders him off or he'll shoot, but it lands on deaf ears. Suddenly, a gunshot tears through the ceiling and a pistol is brought to Forester's head. It was the Chief. Tara is crying and begging for him to stop. He rises and walks over to her and they embrace. The Chief picks up the major from the ground and his face is a bloody pulp. I walk over to check on him, and the major talks through broken teeth and jaw.

        He is the personal assistant to the general in command of Fort Lewis. He was sent down alongside the Colonel to check the area and take command of the purge operation. Which, it turns out the Colonel knew nothing about. The major mumbles more about his hatred for the Colonel and especially the Chief. The Colonel was deployed here, and he was going to meet his maker with a bullet to the back in the middle of a deader swarm. That was the plan. The Colonel was asking too many questions about some plans he saw on the general's desk in his office. Not to mention the rumors the Chief heard going around the post. According to the major, the Colonel is a loose end that needed to be taken care of. The Chief was just a bonus. Forester just stares at the man. Tara still sobbing in his arms, just keeps talking about Jess and Collin. I kneel next to her and ask where they are. She cries more and buries her head in Forester's chest. I look to him, and he is also almost in tears. He motions for me to look behind myself, and I worry about what I'll see.

        I walk over to a corner and I turn and cry. On the ground, are Collin and Jess, holding each other with bullet holes in their heads. I turn to the Major and point my weapon at him. The Chief sees the two and bows his head. Before anything else happens, the Chief slams his bloodied face into a window shattering it. He lifts the major and throws him out the window onto a group of about eight deaders. His screams draw more. The Chief watches as the major is torn to pieces. "Good riddance, jerk." Is all he can say. A thumping up the stairs makes the Colonel and Chief aim their guns. The other two soldiers made it back! The Colonel laughs, and the Chief actually walks up to the two and hugs both. They were able to lead the deaders far enough away and then doubled back. At least something good came out of this, but I can't bring myself to be joyful. Forester is still holding on to Tara, and she is still sobbing. The other four realize what is happening and stop celebrating.

        I seriously long for the day when I don't have to be in this world and more.

Hal's notes

We have a quick burial for the three, thanks to the kindness of the service men. I pray as the two lowest ranking soldiers stand watch. Forester approaches me and says we need to go. I agree. We need to get Tara and move along. Forester puts his hand on my shoulder and lets me know the three of us will be together from now on. The Colonel offers to accompany us to the city limits and I thank him.

Tara stands by her family's graves sobbing. I walk up to her and put an arm around her to help her through this terrible ordeal. She has lost so much, but then again so have the rest of us. I don't understand how people could do what they did to her siblings. Children! It makes me angry enough to shoot the one who did this, but that problem is solved. I let her know we need to leave, and the soldiers are going to help us get to the city limits. We turn and head to our new group to depart. She looks back one more time then whispers, "I'm never coming back here again". Forester, his double bladed axe in one hand, and his chain saw in the other, brings up the rear of our little group.

We leave, and I pray that we will find a better place to help this little girl cope. Maybe, she'll be able to help us along the way too.

July 23
Hal's notes

It has taken the seven of us almost two days to make it to the city limits on foot. We had to hide and stay in various houses along the way. Thank God for these soldiers. We came upon a horde of what looked like a hundred deaders. The two lower ranked men cleared a path, and led us to a safe place. Forester tore into a group of deaders with his chainsaw and axe. The soldiers stood stunned watching him work; hacking and sawing, body parts were literally raining down on the ground. He must have taken out thirty of the dead. I overheard the Chief tell the Colonel, "The General better hope we find him before this guy does. I don't think a nuke could stop him!" The Colonel nodded with a whistle, "You aren't kidding. I'm glad he's on our side." We stop for a short while to get our bearings as the Colonel discusses plans with the other soldiers. The house the corporal found is back from the road enough that we should be safe for a time.

Tara is sleeping, fitfully. I can't imagine what she is feeling or thinking watching her whole family die in front of her. Forester is on the floor next to her, and he looks like he is trying not to cry. I sit next to him and try to make small conversation. Before I can say anything, he sobs out two words that make me stop breathing. "I failed," he chokes out, "I said I'd protect them, I said I'd get them where they needed to be, and I failed. I failed this little girl, I failed her brother and sister, and I failed the guy that saved my life." He bows his head and shakes. "I failed her. I wasn't there and they both died. I left the house, we'd argued about the stupidest thing and I just walked out without telling Lindy I loved her. Let alone good-bye. Then I saw Rhonda in the window waving to me and I ignored her. They'd be with us now if I wasn't such a stupid ass." I look down and see a picture of a very pretty lady hugging a girl that looks about Tara's age. I pat his shoulder, and he gives me a half smile. "I promise, Pastor, I will take care of Tara even if it kills me, and I will take out anyone that tries to hurt her!" I pat him again and tell him to try and rest. This small talk tells me volumes about a man who's lost just as much as Tara. God brought us together. I know it now and my faith is stronger for it.

I approach the Colonel who asks how the others are doing. I tell him about my and Forester's conversation, and he then becomes silent. "The general is going to pay for what he has caused. I will not stop until I find him, Hal," he assures me. "You're not doing it alone, Cal. I'm going with you. I promised your dad I'd keep you safe, and I know what a knuckle-head you are," the Chief said with a big smile. The Colonel smiles back and they return to planning.

It turns out that the Chief is the Colonel's uncle. I would ask for more to learn about these people, but the Colonel tells me I should get some rest. We're moving out in six hours, and he wants us all as ready for anything as possible. I don't argue. I retire to a chair next to Forester and Tara. Both of them asleep. I have made the decision that no matter what, I will see that these two people survive this even if it costs me my life. I'm ready anyways.

Lord, please give me the strength to do your will, and keep my new friends safe. Thank you for restoring me to my desire to serve you faithfully. I promise to do my best to shepherd your children to you, and to hopefully bring an end to this hell on earth.

July 24
Hal's notes

      We arrive at the perimeter the military set up on the edge of town, and it is completely deserted. The two enlisted men make a sweep of the area and give us the "all clear". Forester takes the point for Tara and I as we approach the make shift command base that is set up. The three of us stay close by each other. Forester tells Tara not to wander, and stay close. I believe she may be taking the place of the daughter he lost, but I would rather not pass any judgement. He is a good man, and I'm glad he is our friend.

      The Colonel comes up to the three of us with a set of keys, two full boxes of ammunition and some weapons. He is giving us a jeep. He wants us to have as much of an advantage as possible. He also supplies us with some rations and long range radio so we can keep in contact. We say our good-byes, but before we can load up the Chief wants to talk to me. He lets me know that they're going to work their way back to the base up the freeway. And if we need anything, he is a certified and licensed helicopter pilot. He will get us to safety. I thank him, and before he joins his fellows he whispers something to me that raises my spirits to outer space. I reply, "He is risen indeed!" The Chief turns to me and waves with large grin on his face. He has given me something that we seem to be running in short supply, but it is something that we need.

      Hope.

To: General Thomas Samuels
Joint Chiefs of Staff
United States Army

From: General Thaddeus Morganstein
Department of Defense
United States Marine Corp

Tom,

    The following notes are from a time after the three individuals survived the D.A.V. and left for the eastern part of the state. Satellite imaging can't seem to pick up their whereabouts at this time. Homeland Security is now involving themselves as is the C.I.A., F.B.I., and everyone else that can track down the renegade general. It is turning into a circus since the President authorized these organizations in. Talk about a cluster---never mind.

    The Reverend Hal Jones now determines the days in A.V., or After Virus. According to the notes, they end up somewhere close to Spokane, WA. I'll get a hold of you soon so we can get this problem taken care of without these other jackasses messing it up.

Ted

Hal's notes
1 A. V.

       A new world. I've decided to number our days as "After Virus". Anything from here forward is going to be known as that. That will be the easiest way for me to keep track of days, weeks, years(?) while all of this goes on. Tara is very quiet, and I completely understand. It has taken several hours to reach the Morton/Packwood area, and it is getting dark. The deaders are everywhere. It took so because we actually had to stop for a while as a horde of deaders, too many to count, approached us. We found an empty house and stayed there while we watched them go by. I am certain God was watching us because none of the dead ones noticed us. And there had to be over a thousand. We left, and found an empty motel just off of HWY 12. Forester says he'll sleep in a chair by the door, just in case. We are hoping to be over the pass sometime tomorrow, and make a bee line to our first contact that has part of the formula for the vaccine I hope.

       I believe the stop is somewhere in Wenatchee. Will have to make some kind of base of operations mainly because I'm unsure about how to read the coordinates or latitude and longitude. Forester actually know how to handle the GPS, so I insist he take charge of our little group. He chuckles and tells me to go to sleep. I want to. I'm not sure when we will sleep soundly again, or if we will sleep forever. Please help us to get through this, Heavenly Father. We can't do it without you.

Hal's notes
2 A.V.

       The drive we've had has been uneventful. Before we left the town of Morton, we found as much food as we could fit into the jeep, and still be comfortable. The dead here was not as wide spread. Although, we didn't see any people. It was quite eerie to tell the truth. I visited up here at a new church being opened by a friend from seminary, but he was nowhere to be found, and his church was actually burned to the ground. Instead of taking a chance and possibly putting ourselves in danger, I suggested we go ahead and leave. No matter what, I'll see him again. Most likely on the other side of Heaven.

       We make it to the White Pass ski lodge and decide this will be as good a place as any to stay. Everything looks empty. No sign of life, or dead. That's good I suppose. The main lodge looks the most secure so that is where we'll make our "camp".

       After setting up in a large room with two separate bedrooms, I decide to take the binoculars that were in the jeep and take a look around. Tara decides to stay in the room while I go out. I can tell she is still in shock about the last few days. As I find a high enough place with an unobstructed view, I check our surrounding. Forester is nowhere to be seen, but I know he is close by. Looking east, I see a problem. A horde of about 15 to 20 deaders are heading this way. Fortunately, I see that Forester must have set up a barrier of some kind while we settled in the room. We should be safe, But I wonder how were going to get out of here come tomorrow. After thinking about it, I realize or jeep isn't the quietest car, and that probably drew the deaders here. A doe and two fawn come out of the woods. I can see the doe is bleeding on her leg and can't run. The two fawn do not want to leave her, to their mistake. All three last maybe five minutes, and it is a terrible sight.

       Ah! Forester put his hand on my shoulder and scared me to death! I had no idea he was even near. He laughs and suggests we get inside. It will be dark soon, and he reminds me the dead get a lot more active. To our surprise, Tara has prepared a dinner for us. Canned chili and some garlic bread? I am mildly impressed at what she did and tell her. She gives me a slight smile and thanks me as we sit to eat. She is a lot stronger than I gave her credit for. I hope her resolve stays with her for as long as it can. We may need to lean on her strength too.

Forester wants us to stay another day or two. He wants to make a more detailed plan for when we leave, and I don't disagree. After we leave here, the potential for not getting any kind of rest is great. Tara agrees. She wants to explore the area since she hasn't been here before. I tell her it isn't a good idea with the deaders all over down below. She understands and goes to her room and lays down. I think she and I will go later, if it looks safe enough.

Suddenly, we see movement about fifty yards away. Forester comes running to us and said he sees two girls trapped behind a building with about three deader approaching. One of the girls is hurt, so he is going. decide to help and grab one of the M16s the soldiers gave us, along with his axe. I know there is no way I can keep up with him, but I have to try. Tara decides to help and grabs the pistol. "Stay close," I tell her. We head out.

One of the girl's screams in pain so loud that more deaders start to come from around other lodges. They try to run, but I can see the injured girl is slowing them down too much. They won't make it. Suddenly, Forester appears and starts swinging his axe at the closest dead. They all fall into pieces. He quickly picks up the injured girl and heads our way. I make one shot at a pursuing deader and hit his head. We retreat to our lodging right behind Forester and the two girls.

Denise and Linda are the names of the two young ladies we rescued. They have a group of about eight of them; four boys and four girls counting these two. They said that they were on a trip for a graduation party to Lake Chelan. One of their boyfriend's family owns a house close by, or on the lake. They were "detoured" here when they were heading out. It sounds like the outbreak must have traveled, or began traveling outside of Winlock/Napavine area just before graduation. It certainly didn't take long to get this far. The injured one, Denise, explains this to me as I try to treat her leg. Looking closely at it, she wasn't bitten by a human, but an animal. Great. The virus can cross species. That makes it all the more important we find the people with the vaccine parts.

Denise is already suffering from symptoms of the bite. She is infected, no doubt. I explain to her friend Linda that I've done everything I can. I don't tell her it is just a matter of time, mainly because I don't know the incubation period. I excuse myself and ask Forester if he could give me a hand. Out of the earshot of our two guests, I give Forester the news. He reacts as I expected, insisting we get the two of them out as soon as possible. I reluctantly agree. He offers to get them to their friends right away. "Sorry, father," he says, "its them or us. And I'm not taking any chances with the kid." He retrieves his axe, and informs the girls of the plan. Tara asks me what is going on and why they can't stay. I tell her and she gasps. I ask her not to say anything for her safety sake, and she agrees also reluctantly.

Before Forester leaves, I decide to go along in case he needs back up. Tara with the 9mm says she is also going because she doesn't want to be alone. Before either of us can give her our disapproval, she cocks her weapon and heads out the door. She let us know that we have a clear shot to the building the girls said their group was at. Forester and I look at each other and shrug. He let out a loud "Ha!" and lifts Denise. He is out the door with Linda behind him, and I follow. I hope Denise finds peace quickly and doesn't turn.

Half way to the other building, and things go relatively uneventful. Then Denise starts to moan and get agitated. The virus must be progressing farther and faster than I thought it would. As a doctor this virus is fascinating and would make an exciting research project, and as a person I feel bad for her and what kind of pain she must be going through. Being a pastor, this man-made abomination is abhorrent.

Now Denise is getting louder. Too loud for any of us to be safe. Tara grabs my arm tightly, and it hurts. She is getting scared that we aren't going to make it. We can hear the movement of shuffling feet around us, and Forester gives me a look that he wants to drop the girl and run. Linda is trying to calm her, but she just screams louder. Then we see numerous deaders approaching, and Forester is left with no choice. He drops her and moves next to Tara. Linda starts to freak out and scream about her friend, but it is too late. She is gone. Forester grabs Linda and heads for the building with Tara and I right on his heels. As he runs he takes the head off two of the dead and doesn't even break stride. Tara and I struggle to keep up, although she is having an easier time than I. By the time we are within ten feet of the building, Denise is standing and plodding toward us. With the blank eyes of the soulless horrors that chase us.

We get inside the lodge and Linda falls into the arms of a boy named Marcus. We tell them what happened and what we had to do to save ourselves. Another young man named Austin loses control and attacks Forester for what he did to his girlfriend. Forester is actually caught off guard for a second before retaliating. The boy was built like a high school football player. Obviously worked out, but Forester is at least six foot nine, close to 300 pounds of muscle and has been known to lift logs with his bare hands when they've fallen on the ground. At least that is what someone told me at the high school when we first met. The boy doesn't last five seconds.

Tara aims her pistol and warns the others she'll shoot if anyone else tries anything. They decide to listen to the thirteen-year-old and stay still. I offer condolences for their loss, and wished I could've done more, but the only answer we get is from Austin. He promises we will pay for what happened. We decide to leave.

We get back to our lodge room and reinforce our barricade. We may have just made another problem with the seven remaining in the other building. Forester looks at us both and says we leave at first light tomorrow, and he suggests we try to rest.

It is after midnight and Forester is still watching out the window at the other building, when the quiet of the night is shattered by the sound of an abandoned car exploding.

Tara runs into the room in a panic. I tell her to get her things and be ready to go at a moment's notice. If this group of people are that anxious to kill us they may blow up a car right next to us and take out the whole lodge. We head to the back balcony hoping we can slip down to the lower floor. Not possible. The deaders are all over the place. They must have found a way in. Another explosion. Fortunately, the deader go to it. Some of them fall over the side of the lower balcony and their heads completely shatter when they hit the ground. Forester shows up with a rope to lower us. Tara is a little scared to do this, but she realizes it is a matter of life and death. Including being a walking dead.

Forester gets us down there with little to no trouble. He is truly amazing. He practically leaps down to us and we run for the back stairs to the jeep. As we get down to the ground, Forester takes a different route. Why? We need to stay together, and his leaving upsets Tara greatly. I think he is going to put a stop to the people trying to kill us. I don't think they realize that these explosions are going to draw more of the dead to us. Providing that there are more.

We round the building to find two of the seven standing by the jeep. One of them climbs in then gets out swearing. "No keys," he says between curses. From nowhere a deader grabs the potential driver and bites into his face. His screams draw more to them while the other attempts to help his friend, he too is overwhelmed.

Another explosion as a car bursts into flames. They've got to be throwing some kind of match into the gas tanks. Then more deaders show up. Where are they all coming from? A scream from one of the girls we rescued. We see Linda running and her clothes are on fire. She stops, drops and rolls but it does her no good. She is soon overcome by at least ten zombies. Tara covers her ears to drown out her screams. We approach the jeep and Tara throws up at the sight of what's left of the two trying to steal the it.

Still no sign of Forester when I turn to try and find him. I'm suddenly tackled by a deader and end up on the ground struggling. He tries to bite me but I'm able to push him off. He proves a little faster than I and is on his feet first. The back of his head suddenly explodes and he falls to the ground unmoving. Behind him I see Tara literally holding the smoking gun and shaking.

We need to find Forester and get out of here now.

I stand and approach Tara; carefully pushing her gun to point downward and putting the safety on. Unlike her siblings, this is the first time she has actually fired her weapon and killed something. Even though the creature was already dead, it still makes her uneasy. To put it mildly. I thank her and she immediately throws up. I actually hope that she always responds like this and does not become desensitized to the killing. Suddenly a familiar sound erupts! We see Forester swinging his chainsaw cutting, mangling, decapitating, and disintegrating deaders by the dozens. He reminds me of Samson and the Philistines; when Samson took the jaw bone of the ass and slew the 1000 of them every time he swung it. I picture him looking like Forester, but with longer hair.

Forester doesn't see the deader behind him. I take aim with my M16 and fire. The head explodes as Forester turns to see the body fall. He looks to us and waves, leaving his "Philistines" to stumble and miss grabbing him. As we begin to get into the jeep, Tara is grabbed by a deader at the same time Forester catches up with us. He grabs the zombie's head and completely pulls it off the body and watches it slump into a pile. We quickly board the jeep and leave this place behind without a look back.

4 A.V.

We are able to make it as far as Wenatchee before we run out of fuel. I thought we had more, but I guess I was mistaken. The motel we find has two floors, must be a "6", and we quickly find two adjoining rooms for the day. I'm hoping we can stay here maybe a couple of days to rest and make a better plan for finding the people with the vaccine ingredients. As we fortify our two rooms, my mind travels back a few hours to White Pass. I did not see the boy Austin in the confusion. He may have survived, but I doubt it. The problem is if he did, he will certainly try to follow us and attempt to finish what he started. Just one more thing to worry about, besides food, water, gas, and any other necessity we'll need. The living are proving be worse to deal with than the dead.

With the stairs barricaded, we finally feel safe enough to try and get some rest. Forester heads out to scavenge. I don't fight it as he leaves. Tara, bless her heart, has already claimed a bed and is sleeping. I think I'll follow her lead and do the same. I leave the door between the rooms open giving both of us a little privacy but still able to hear each other if one of us is in trouble.

5 A.V.

      I guess the soldiers were right. I wasn't completely positive how far the deaders had gotten, but the town is crawling with them. Tara and I venture out from the motel, but not too far. Around here are a few stores that look promising. Except, I don't want to get our hopes up. The population in Wenatchee was probably at least as big if not bigger than the entirety of Lewis County, not just Winlock. I'm almost certain whatever passed the virus on in town spread quickly from Napavine then outward north, east, and south to rest of the county in hours. From there it just went exponential.

      We make it to the department store close by. It is good sized and we start hunting. It is fairly empty, but we find some useful items. Two machetes with carrying cases, a propane stove and some small canisters of propane, and a couple of belts to put the machetes around our wastes. We work our way to the grocery side of this store, but I lose sight of Tara. Ah, there she is. And she is staring intently at the machete I gave her.

      Tears start coming down as I imagine she is thinking of her family and Collin. The machete probably reminds her of him. I feel for her, we've all lost so much, but at her age. I decide against any more foraging today and approach Tara. She looks up at me still crying, and I put my arm around her. We leave.

      She doesn't deserve this. None of us do. I look up to God to ask, but before I say anything, a crack of thunder with drops of rain. We hustle back to the rooms. I'm certain we have food for a few days, but we will need more soon.

      The rain comes down hard with thunder and lightning coming in two minute intervals. I haven't seen this kind of storm since my visit to the Midwest. It was just before a tornado touched down, but fortunately it didn't. I wonder how Forester is doing right now in this? He has been gone for quite a while, and Tara is concerned. I am also, but she sits at the window watching for his return. I won't discourage her. As long as it takes her mind off of her family. But, I pray Forester is alright. He has been gone for hours now. I wonder where he could have gotten off to?

I was able to get Tara to try and sleep, but I know it was tough for her. We're both worried about Forester and pray he is okay. We are planning another trip to the store now that it is morning to try and find some more food. Before we leave she points my attention to four people running. Because of that we're positive they are not deaders. They duck behind a gas station, and then sprint to the other side of it just beyond a trio of cars. An RV is close and they try to get into it. They can't. I can now see why they were running. About two dozen deaders are not far from them. Since they can't run, I don't believe they'll catch the four unless something happens to make them stop. And something does. They become boxed in by another group of about 20 coming toward them from the opposite direction. We decide to help.

She with her pistol, and I the M16, head to the railing of the floor we are on. I take a shot at a deader about ten yards from them, and end up taking down two. No time to get cocky, I fire again and down another, causing some to trip on them as they fall. Tara waves to get their attention, and it works. The head to us. Tara gets over our makeshift barricade to lead them up here. I remind her of being cautious and she gives me the look that every teenager gives their parents the "Duh, I know, "look.

One of them trips, a woman, behind the other three. A man, and two teenage boys stop. The older man tells the two boys to keep running as he goes back to help the woman. I fire again and hit another zombie that is almost on top of them. The man gets the woman up and they hurry to catch the two boys. They all four make it none the worse and all of us get into other rooms and bring out as much furniture as we can to block the stairs.

They made it. That is the good news. The bad news is there is an enormous hoard of deaders heading toward us. I hope our make-shift barricade works.

7 A.V.

After everyone has gotten a good nights' sleep, or what passes for it now, we reconvene in Tara's and my room. Introductions are made, and then we share small amount of food. The Stiegers, Wes, Jan, Tyler and Don are eternally grateful for their rescue. We don't tell them everything about us mainly because we're not sure we can trust them. Although, they seem on the level and I'm going to try and give them the benefit of the doubt.

I am getting greatly concerned about Forester. He has been gone for at least two days, and I'm unsure if he is even alive. Watching Tara stare out the window, I can tell she feels the same. I pray for his safe return. The herd of dead have completely surrounded the motel we are in. At first there were only what looked like a couple dozen or so. Now, there are hundreds filling the parking lot, and the back of the building we are in. Our make shift barricade is still holding, thank God, but all of us are not positive it will last forever. Also, how will Forester get to us? If they make it through the barrier, we won't last a minute.

Suddenly, the building shakes like an earthquake. We all look out the window and see a plume of smoke rising from an explosion a few blocks away. We all look at each other as Tara grabs my hand. Wes says they haven't seen anyone for weeks, and the other three concur. I certainly hope it isn't that Austin. The deaders are drawn to the noise and begin to leave. The Stiegers' thank us again and decide to leave since they have an opportunity to run. I try to dissuade them, but they choose to go. I ask to pray for them, and they allow it. The deaders have cleared out being curious about the noise except for a few stragglers. Before the family leaves, Tara hands Wes her 9mm with the ammo. He is speechless, and they leave.

I smile at her, feeling very proud that she would give up her weapon to a family she hardly knew. I guess she could be a better judge of character than I thought. She is caring, and compassionate, and I feel if anyone makes it out of this mess she will. Now if Forester would hurry and get back so we can try to leave. I think we've over stayed our welcome.

It is the middle of the night and I hear shuffling on the walk-way just outside the room. Tara also hears it and is by my side in seconds. I grab the M16, and as quietly as possible, I tip toe to the window and pull back the shade. I get my hopes up thinking it could be Forester. As does Tara, but we are shot down as we see three or four deaders wandering out on the walkway between rooms. Somehow the dead have circumvented the barricade at the stairs. Now we have a problem.

The door to the room that Tara came from is open. We need to close it and secure it quickly before they find a way in. Hopefully we can barricade ourselves in here and pray they move on. I head to the door, but Tara doesn't want me to leave her. I reassure her I'm just going to seal the door the best I can and I'm coming right back. I tell her to head to the bathroom and lock herself in. Before she can move, and I get to the door, I get spotted. The shades in the other room weren't closed. No ones' fault. Neither one of us thought any of the deaders would get pass our stack of furniture at the head of the stair. The deader that spotted me violently attacks the window coming through it with a loud crash. I hear Tara scream and quickly slam the door shut. I try to put something in front of it as I hear the deaders stumbling through the other room. We retreat to the bathroom and lock the door. Tara curls up into a ball in the corner of the tub and starts to shake. I stand in front of her aiming the gun at the door. I pray and ask God to make our end swift. I don't tell her, but if they get through this door, I'm not going to let her suffer. I will make sure the dead don't get her.

We both prepare for the worst when we hear a loud thunk. Soon a voice barrels out, "Come on you suns' of bitches. You're not getting my friends!" We then hear what sounds like flesh being ripped apart. I open the door and it is Forester! I grab a machete and go to help, but he doesn't need it. His axe is coming down from head to crotch of one of the deades, splitting it in uneven halves. In his other hand, he has a female deader by the throat and is throwing her into the wall, squashing its head like an over ripe grapefruit. He gets hold of one more and rips it in half right at the waste. He stomps the head flat and throws the rest to the other side of the room.

Forester insist we leave right now. We don't hesitate and grab our belongings. Tara though grabs hold of him and makes him grunt a little from the pain of her hug. He smiles and hugs her back letting her know that there will be time to do this later. We grab our belonging and head out. A small problem. Our jeep is out of fuel. Forester says he has it covered and points to an SUV that looks brand new. We load up and hit the road. A very nice Escalade, with a full tank of gas and extra in the back. I don't ask where it came from, or where he has been. At least not yet. I am just grateful he is alive.

9 A.V.

I slept after we left Wenatchee, and I have no idea how far we've gone. The sun is up and is getting warm. Eastern Washington gets extremely warm in the summer, and very cold in the winter. By the position of the sun I'm thinking it is still morning. Forester says he actually stopped at an out of the way place that was safe and slept for a few hours. We've only been actually traveling for a shorter time than I figured. I'm glad forester got some rest. Before I can ask him, he tells me what he was doing before he got back to us.

He said he was looking for food and fuel so we could keep moving. As he was searching he heard what sounded like crying. Forester hid and watched an interesting parade. A group of about five women was marching four teenage boys down the street. Despite all the noise and wailing they were making, the deaders were few and not a threat. All the boys were in chains, and scared to death he said. One of the women released one of the boys and quickly shoved a knife into his neck. The others quickly pulled cups out and filled them with blood and started to drink. I am disgusted by the depravity that people have sunk to in this environment. Forester starts to describe some other things they were doing with the boys, but I stop him. I don't want to hear anymore.

Thinking he needed to get back soon, he leaves them to continue his search. Traveling a couple more blocks he was almost overcome by a huge horde of zombies. Fortunately, he made it to a second floor of a close building. Otherwise we wouldn't be having this conversation. Night was coming so he decided to lay low for a while. He heard noise coming from another room on the floor he was at, and discovered two brothers in their twenties covered in blood. Even though he could see the fear in their eyes as he entered, they calmed when Forester offered them water.

Both of them are sweating, but shivering with an occasional convulsion. Then Forester notices the blood with teeth marks on the arm of one, and the same on the leg of the other. The taller of the two boys is cradling the other. Looking at them it wouldn't be long before both turned, and the two boys know it. Forester offers to help them not to turn. Neither could bring themselves to end it, and they agree to his gift.

The silence in the room is deafening. Forester knows what people think of him, but they'd be wrong. He hates what he is becoming in this new world. Both pass, and Forester gives them the mercy they requested. I feel as he does. I am feeling the need to end the lives of the evil men who caused this, but it is not my place to judge. God forgive me for my anger. Yet I see no other recourse to punish these people, and it scares me to think that I'm considering even attempting something that I've preached against.

An hour or so later we stop in a residential area for the rest of the day. All of us are feeling the weight of the environment, and what it is doing to our bodies. And our souls. The place we are at is a gated community so it is relatively clear of deaders. After we get in we make sure and block the gate as best we can and search for lodging. I'm starting to wonder if the manufactured virus wasn't started in Winlock and sent to other parts of the state. It seemed to spread fast, and something about it is nagging the back of my mind. Just one more thing to stress about I guess.

We find a decent place to rest for our time here, and fortunately there seems to be power to this area. Forester points out the solar panels on a hill side that is probably what is keeping this place going. The house seems secure enough, but we will take extra precautions. Our relaxation is cut short when we hear noise coming from another room. Forester raises his axe, and I the M16. Out of the room comes an average sized dog wagging its tail. But behind the pup is a girl about Tara's age with a baseball bat.

I lower my weapon and approach trying to defuse the situation. She calms down, Forester relaxes his stance, but still has a white knuckle hold of his axe. I offer the girl some water and she thanks me. She sits on the closest chair to take a deep breath. Suddenly she begins to break down and sob. We introduce ourselves to help the girl calm down. Her name is Tina, and she relates her story as best she can.

Tina was with her parents waiting for the military to get out of the city to somewhere safe. Two "soldiers" came into the house and began ransacking the house. Both were armed, and one of them hit Tina's father knocking him to the ground. Her mother told her to run and she did. She hid herself in a closet or something and waited. All she heard was the two men beating on her parents. Her mom begs them to stop, and then she hears a gun shot. Tina's mom screams, and then a slap knocking her to the ground. What happens next is too much for her and she begins to tremble at what she heard. I tell her it is alright, but she wants to continue. One more gunshot then silence. She comes out of her hiding place to see her parents in a pool of blood. Not to mention in a state that makes her vomit. They begin to move and runs to hide again, trying to be quiet. A voice from outside makes her folks turn to the noise and lumber toward it. She peeks out to see her parents assault and begin to eat the owner of the voice. Tina then loses it again.

Forester is enraged. He wants to find these two and make them pay, but I remind him that the chances of them being alive is extremely thin. We would be better pressed to secure the house and stay close to where we are. If he left, he may not make it back this time. He agrees as we head to the SUV and get our supplies. Tara stays with Tina and helps her calm down, and they begin to chat. It is good for her to have someone her own age to talk to. We return with the things and proceed to board up windows. Tomorrow, Forester wants to explore, but I just think he wants to find the two "soldiers". As evening comes we find some canned food in the house, and since there is still power, we make ourselves a hot meal.

The girls decide to stay together in one room. Probably to make themselves feel safe, or just to talk some more. Forester offers me the master bedroom to rest. I don't try to change his mind because he wants to stay by the door just in case. He then offers to finish his story about the brothers. He didn't want to talk about it in front of Tara because of what he did. The brother who was in the worst shape passed as Forester was watching the deaders out the window. He turned to see the older brother crying, and was just about to end both of them as the "dead" one bit a huge chunk of flesh off of his face. Two swings of his axe and Forester gives them the mercy he promised. He shudders a little after his story. Probably thinking about what he did to the two boys. Then he talks about the high school, and what he did there. That was nothing because he felt justified for those military people were gunning down unarmed people. He was not going to allow it to happen to us. I think his adrenaline was pumping at such a high rate that he didn't think. Just acted.

When he was leaving he found a backpack with some food and water in it. When he approached the motel and saw the deaders surrounding it, he knew that he had to act quickly. Seeing a gas station not far away he made a snap decision to cause an extreme distraction. Finding a working lighter, he went to work. The explosion worked as he hoped. Drawing the deaders from the motel. Forester watched the four people running from our room as he made it back to rescue us from our predicament. Losing all that fuel was probably not the smartest thing he could've done, but I tell him I would have done the same thing.

10 A.V.

Tara is not happy. Forester has decided to go and look for the two men who pretended to be soldiers and kill Tina's parents. First of all, Tara reminds him that may not even be alive. What makes her more upset is I'm going with him. I showed her how to use the M16 so it is staying here. Forester has his axe, chain saw, and I grabbed one of the two machetes we found back in Wenatchee. I promise that we will return in a day, whether we find the two or not. Since we've been at Tina's house there have maybe been about five deaders that have passed by, and that was in the span of several hours. As long as the girls stay as quiet as possible, they'll be okay.

Tina had the idea to video the two jerks with her phone. Since the power hasn't shut down here yet she has been able to keep it charged. Hoping for a phone call that will never come. Forester and I watch the video and zoom in on the two faces of the men. For their sake, they better be dead. I don't even want to think what Forester is going to do to them. If they actually are military, they might have a slight advantage over us with their training, but then I think a little more and they don't have a chance. Forester told me when Tara was resting in the back of the jeep before we got to Wenatchee about how he used to hunt and what. Bear, elk, deer, and the occasional cougar. It was how he hunted that made me give him a double take. He said he used a knife to kill a bear, a bow against a cougar, and a spear to take down an elk.

Funny thing though. I believe him. His tale is too fantastic to not be true. And if you met him, you'd almost think he did all that with his bare hands. His story of watching the building in Winlock being filled with lab equipment was certainly true. So how could this not be? Forester has worked in the wood since the age of thirteen, so his story isn't that surprising.

Why am I joining him on this manhunt? After our adventure a few days ago, I want to make sure he makes it back. I also want to see the twisted individuals who think what they are doing is acceptable just because of the current state of everything. Tara hugs me, and is in tears. I reassure her that we'll be back before she knows it. She hugs Forester and tells him that she is afraid to lose either one of us. She doesn't want any more of her family to die. Forester picks her up and tells her nothing on Earth will stop him or us from coming back to her.

No doubt will be back. Not because of my faith, which is a huge part of it, but because of how he said it. There is no way he is going to let this young lady down that the two of us have become attached to. Nor am I.

As we leave the house I decide it would be best if we bring Tina with us. Before I can say anything to Forester he tells me the exact thing I'm thinking. We both agree that it would be a good thing for Tara since and neither of us could stand to leave her here on her own. A grocery store is close by and right next to it is a liquor store. Stumbling out the front door with no regard for their safety is the two men that killed Tina's parents. There are a few deaders around, but not too many that we couldn't handle without guns.

These two geniuses are taunting the dead with words. Then they throw their empty booze bottle at the deaders, but completely miss. They both laugh so hard they almost fall down. It is a good thing the zombies can't, or just won't run. Otherwise as drunk as they are, they'd couldn't have gotten more than five feet. All the alcohol in the world won't take away any of the pain Forester is going to inflict on them.

Forester is going to try to use stealth instead of barreling into them like a runaway freight train. He wants me to stay back just in case. I believe he is worried for my safety, but he shouldn't. I tell him he should pull ahead to keep pace with the two and I'll follow best I can. He is surprisingly fast for a man his size, and I don't think I could keep up with him on my best day.

I'm not sure I can kill anyone like he thinks he is capable. Taking out the dead is different. They are all soulless shells that have only one need. To feed on the living. Even after what those two men did to Tina's parents I'm not sure I can take their lives. I would like to beat them to bloody pulps, but even that is against what the Bible says. And I don't want to compromise my faith even though we are in this terrible environment. If push came to shove, I'm certain I'd do whatever I had to too protect my new family.

Avoiding the deaders isn't proving too difficult. They are focusing on the noise the two belligerent drunks are making. That way it is easier for me to almost keep pace with Forester. This is fascinating though. From a scientific viewpoint. To study how these creatures are able to move around after being dead. What is exactly is their driving force? How is the brain able to function, let alone the nervous systems, to make motor functions possible? Plus, the necropsy, muscle atrophy, and I actually watched one deader's arm just fall off. He just kept plugging along. As a doctor, or a man of science, this would be an interesting experiment. As a pastor, it is totally an abomination. But still……

I move closer and I see Forester has made it to the top of a bus without being spotted. I get a little closer and wonder what will happen next. Forester ready's his chain saw to bring down on the fools who dared became one of his targets. I start to say a quick prayer for them then the unthinkable happens.

Forester has slipped off the bus and landed hard. Even from this distance I can see that he is hurt and not moving. The bang of his saw and axe has alerted the so-called soldiers and they are turning back to the bus. But the deaders have heard it too, and are heading right for him. I reach for my gun, but I remember leaving it with Tara. This is not good.

I yell and holler to get everyone's attention. The dead and the soldiers see me, and I get a few to follow me including the two "soldiers". They shoot wildly in my direction which attracts more of the deaders to join them. What they plan to do to me, and then kill me chills me to the bone. I look and Forester is up and moving. He is dazed but I think he is fine. He quickly gets into the bus and shuts the door before he becomes an early dinner. I make it inside a building, but I'm unsuccessful in closing the door. More bullets zip past my head as I duck down and run to the end of the closest hallway. The men are still yelling and screaming, and I can hear the deaders behind them. I need to figure out a way to leave here and trap them inside with the zombies. I find a room with a window facing the street where the bus is, but no sign of Forester. Either he is unconscious or worse. I will help him after I get away from these two maniacs and the horde following them.

An emergency fire hose! I break the glass case, pull the hose and brace myself. I find a corner that allows me to see from two directions. Thankful that I can't be approached from behind I wait. A minute. Then two. Soon I think it has been an hour before I hear the group on my tail. I see the first one round the corner firing behind him. The sound of a click-click tells me his gun is finally empty. I don't hesitate as I let loose a torrential flood against my- would- be killer and he flies back into his friend. They both fall hard as they slide into a group of ten deaders knocking them over. But the dead prove to be a little quicker than two drunks. All I hear is their screams as I make a dash for a stair well that leads back to the street. I end up on the other side of the building, and I run as fast as I can back to Forester.

In the bus he is still down, but awake. He asks me about the two men, and I let him know they will never bother anyone again. I help him up and he sees the group of deaders in the building I just escaped from. Looks at me, and he leans on me as I try to help him out of the bus. He took quite a blow falling the ten to twelve feet from the top of the bus. I'm pretty sure he has a concussion. I will have to give him a thorough going over when we get back to the house. We retrieve his saw and axe.

Suddenly, one of the two men come rushing out of the building covered in blood. We both can see he has been bitten several times, but he still swears to kill us before he dies. I'm holding the chain saw, but I can't do anything while I'm holding up Forester. I don't have to. He throws his axe like it is hatchet, and it splits the man's head in half. He falls, never having to worry about becoming a zombie.

Forester rests while I get his axe, and I let him know that he impresses me more and more with his ability. He lets me know he thought I was a goner when the deaders and the other two followed me into the building, and there was nothing he could do to help. He pats my back and lets me know that I impressed him.

It isn't fun when he does it, but I'm glad he is able to. This man has become like a brother to me, and there is no way I'm going to let him, or Tara, die.

11 A.V.

Forester is recovering from his fall. I did give him a quick exam and he does have a slight concussion. He wants to get up and take care of things, but I remind him that not taking it easy for at least a day or two is going to end up worse for him. He relents, and ends up falling to sleep in less than two minutes. The girls and I head to the other room to avoid any unnecessary noise. We don't want to disturb him. I would like Forester to get a lot better before we leave. He needs to be at his best. All of us do, and I think we've gotten the best sleep we're going to get. Tara and Tina go to another room and either play a board game or something. I can hear them laughing which is good.

I step outside remembering to bring a machete and the M16. It finally dawns on me what I did. I essentially caused the two men to die when I used the fire hose on them. My decision to cause their deaths is starting to weigh on me. In my teachings I've always taught what the Savior said. Turn the other cheek. But instead I killed them. I feel like such a hypocrite. I hate what the world is doing to me. I've preached be in the world not of it, and I'm becoming of it to survive. Turning into the person I never wanted to be. It gets harder every day to live in a way that is pleasing to God, but what do I do? I fall to my knees and weep.

Tara sees me and comes out. She puts her arms around me and tells me everything will be fine. I just tell her what I did, and she hugs me harder. She says, "You did what you had to do to save Forester and yourself. Nothing you do would change the way we feel about you. I'm glad you did that for us. I hope I can do the same when I have to." My pride for this girl knows no bounds. Here she has lost more than Forester and myself; yet she is trying to comfort me. I stand and kiss her forehead thanking her. Except the smile I have quickly disappears. A group of about five deaders has spotted us. They are making their way into the yard, and the commotion is drawing a larger group of what looks like twenty-five more to help them out.

We quickly hurry back inside and slam the door! The windows are boarded up, but the chain isn't going to last for long. I tell Tina to get Forester up to head up stairs. She runs as Tara and I put a large table in front of the door. Looking to my right I notice something I haven't seen before. A liquor cabinet. I grab as many bottles as I can carry, and follow Tara. Forester is still a little light headed, but he heads upstairs with the girls. Finding the master bedroom, we jam the door shut with dressers, a night stand, even the bed. I look outside a window to maybe find a way to escape. Then I get another idea.

I find a lighter next to a small bag of pot? Really? Anyways, I take some of the most flammable clothing I can find, and head to the roof. Tara screams at me but I keep going. There is a master bath right in there also, and I tell the girls to find some rubbing alcohol. The room is at the front of the house giving a full view of the front yard. Including the parade of zombies trying to enter it. Sticking a piece of cloth inside the alcohol, I light it. I am directly above about five deaders and I drop it. Two of them burst into flames and fall away from the house to the middle of the yard. Others hearing the commotion come outside to see what all the fuss is. I stick more cloth into a vodka bottle, hoping to God it is flammable, and it is. Several more deaders have caught fire and are reacting to the pain. I thought for sure they couldn't feel anymore. I cross the top of the roof back to the room and grab the machete. Tara pleads with me to not do what she thinks I'm going to do. I smile and tell her to take care of everything till I get back. She cries, thinking she's seen the last of me.

I make my way back out to the roof over to the other side. I find a quick egress to the ground, and work my way around the side to the front. At least eleven of the deaders have succumbed to my make-shift bombs. Then I go to work. I hack, swinging the blade, and cutting off arms. I then realize my error and aim for the necks. I take out two with one swing as I back pedal to avoid getting grabbed. Two more go down as I swing wildly. I'm not sure how many are left, but I will not let them get to the others. I run a short distance allowing three to get closer. They become shorter as I remove their heads. Five more are making their way toward me as I pull away from them to small shed with wood in it. I climb on it, praying I can maintain my momentum to keep on destroying these monsters. Another goes down. Then another. I feel like it is almost over when I slip and tumble to the other side of the shed. Dazed, I hear the remainder coming at me. I am out of chances as I'm surrounded.

Then I hear a sound I wasn't expecting. I look up and see the end of a chain saw cut four zombies in half and fall. This mountain of a man swings again taking out at least six more. He reaches down and pulls me up like I'm a rag doll. We stand back to back as more deaders come at us. His saw in one hand and his axe in the other, he takes out five to every two that I slice. The carnage we do continues for what seems like hours. It feels that way to me. As the deaders finally go from what seemed like dozens to just three, Forester finally falters. His injury is catching up with him after his little rush of adrenaline. I dispatch the rest, and quickly get us back into the house. Both girls greet us with tears and hugs. Scared that we weren't coming back. But we did. Then Tara royally chews me out for being reckless. Not thinking about how I'd get out of this and such. It is hard not to smile, and that just makes her even more angry. She finally calms down and sits. I check Forester to make sure he's alright. He is a little bit dizzy, but I think he'll be fine. I thank him, but he just waves me off. "All part o' the job, Padre," he says with a smile. I get him to return to bed and rest. I make the decision that we need to get out of here within the next few days. Forester salutes me with a yes sir and heads off. Tina double checks the door then heads off to bed. Tara looks at me with her mad look still, but quickly smiles. She hugs me good night, and then gives me a warning, "Don't ever do that again. If you go out and die just because you think you're saving us, I'll kill ya." She walks away smiling, and I laugh myself to sleep.

I'm up early today. I actually beat the sun rise and decide a brief constitutional outside is just what the doctor ordered. Since I'm the doctor, I take my own advice and head out. As I'm leaving, Tina catches up with me. A very nice and gracious host she is for allowing us to stay in her home. We only go as far as the front gate and look into the street. Surprisingly, it is quite empty. All the deaders we can see are more than eight or nine blocks distant. Probably more like six, but I hope for the former. Tina asks me if I've seen the dog she had when we first got here. Come to think of it, I haven't. She wants to look for it, but I don't believe it is a good idea. She practically begs; telling me how it has been her only friend since her parents, and it has warned her of the deaders approaching. I relent, but I make her come in with me while I get at least a machete.

We head out, trying to keep our footsteps as quiet as possible. We don't want any unneeded attention from the local "populace". After about fifteen minutes, we spot the dog. She gets excited and runs to it. Except there's something not right. The way it is walking, dragging its back left foot, and the tail is a bloody stump. I catch her just before she reaches the mutt. She calls to it, and it turns. Half the flesh on the face is gone along with a chunk of the rib cage. Internal organs are hanging out as it works its way toward us. She lets out a cry, but I quickly cover her mouth before we receive any more walking dead. Tina falls to her knees in tears as the dog tries to come for us. The noises it makes are quite disconcerting as I put it down with the machete. I'm glad we only had to go a couple blocks to find out its' fate. I lift her up and start walking her back to the house while she is sobbing. I apologize for putting my hand on her mouth, but she knows I did it to keep us safe. Then we hear the most unexpected sound since all of this started.

Motorcycles. Loud ones like Harleys heading right for us. I know they saw us because we were in the middle of the street. I grab her hand and we make like gang busters to the other side of the street between houses. No reason to give them an idea of where we go to hide. They pass the street where we found the dog, then double back toward us. I only see two, but they look like the bikers that will do whatever they want, and they say it. "All we want is the girl," the bald one says. Apparently he wanted all his hair on his chin. It has to be a foot long. The other one chimes in, "We'll let ya go free, buddy, we just want the girl for-" ……. I don't want to write what they said they were going to do to Tina. Had I the M16, they wouldn't be riding out of here. Or anywhere else ever again. The only way they could have seen us is with binoculars. The one with the hair, is walking around the street making other comments. Loudly. One pulls a gun and starts shooting! They are going to get themselves killed. The house we made it into is maybe twenty feet from them.

Movement. I turn and see a deader coming right at us, and Tina screams. I dispatch it as fast as possible, but our troubles get worse. The two bikers found us. I know because I feel his pistol at the base of my skull.

We are led outside and separated. The bald one grabs Tina and shoves her on the ground. The other matted hair one grabs me around the throat and puts the gun to my head and actually draws blood. Then, the bald one starts to undo his-no! She is just a little girl! Try as I might, I can't get free. The one holding the gun to my head lets me know when his fiend is done with her, he and I are going to have a date.

I react. I fling my head back and can hear his nose brake as I get free. He screams as I get loose and throw myself at the bald one. He is much heavier than I because of his "beer gut", so he throws me to the side like I'm a toy. The other is up, bloody nose and all cussing up a blue streak. Tina crawls over to me and we can do nothing. I look down and start to pray when the one with bloodied nose starts wailing in pain. I look up and he has nothing but a bloody stump where his gun hand was. Not far I see Forester's axe! The bald one turns to defend himself but it is too late. Forester grabs him by the cheeks and turns his head completely around! The sickening crack of the spinal column makes Tina cringe. The other man is holding what's left of his stump of a wrist as Forester applies the same neck twist to him. Forester gets his axe and we head back to the house. I know I told him to stay put, but I'm glad he ignored "doctor's orders."

Tina is pretty shaken up, but okay. She did get a small scrape when she was thrown down, but it was superficial. The cut I got from the gun being pressed up to my head isn't bad. It just looks worse than it actually is. My nurse, Tara, tells me what happened as she fixes my wound. They both heard the motorcycles go past, and one of the guys shooting his gun. Forester gets up, despite his injury and grabs his axe. Tara wants to join him, but he tells her no. It might be worse than we think, and he wants her safe. He promised to be back in ten minutes, except it took him thirteen. He found us and took care of our predicament with extreme prejudice. We're safe, and that is all that matters. I guess he is much tougher than I thought with his injury he got falling off the bus.

Tomorrow, I am going to suggest we start making plans to head to the Idaho/ Washington border. Hopefully, we can be out of here soon.

12 A.V.

        I know it has we've been here longer than planned, but I just want to make sure Forester is at 100%. He is moving around a lot more; checking the boarded windows, fixing doors, and even walking around outside securing the fence. He has been on the roof twice now looking around for any other maniacs. I feel bad he had to get up and save Tina and I. What an awesome man. I hope he accepts the gift God has for him, and Tina too. Forester came into the house after his little "recon" mission to make plans for heading to the border. I suggest the girls put in their two cents worth also because what we decide could literally mean life or death for any one of us. He agrees, and we call them in to plan.

        Neither of us is sure how far away Idaho is from here. Just that it is east. I thought about hitting one of the closer little gas station stores to see if they had a map. Forester said that was a no go. The noise the two bikers made drew tons of deaders to this area. We're lucky they haven't found us yet. It's just a matter time. I believe the plan is to leave tomorrow. We'll load up the SUV today, and try to get to sleep early. Hopefully, we'll be able to leave at day break. Tara asked Forester how he knows that there are so many deaders around. He tells us he went out early one morning just before sunrise to a close by store for a few supplies. That's when he saw them. Though he didn't count them, he thought there had to be at least 120 or so. It wasn't worth it to go hunt for a map just to go maybe a couple hours away. Besides, there should be enough signs around for us to follow that lead to Idaho.

        We all agree on a good time to leave. I ask Tina if her shower is working. I know the toilet is so I thought maybe it could be. She says yes, and I suggest we all take one before we leave. We may not get another chance. The girls start to gather things together as I prepare our last meal here. I can just imagine what is going through Tina's head right now. This is probably the only home she has ever known. Much like Tara. I hope she'll be okay.

13 A.V.

It's hard to tell what time it is. I know it is early, because the sun is just coming up. Forester is already up, and loaded what food we have left. Even after his fall, he is the first one up, checking outside, and making sure we are safe. He smiles at me and lets me know that he is fine. I can see he is a little sore, but I know for a fact that he is probably the toughest man I've ever met. We finish loading together and the girls are up ready to leave. After a quick breakfast we start to leave. Tina does what I thought she would do. She grabs a photo of her parents and starts to cry. I feel for her. The only good thing I have going for me is I lost my wife to cancer about three years ago. Not good, but at least she doesn't have to be in this world now. I also know I will see her again.

Before I can do my pastoral duties, Tara puts her arm around Tina and leads her out to the car. I hear tell of her family, but now she has a new family that will love her just as much. She really is a blessing to have along.

We've been driving for barely an hour when the girls decide they need a bathroom break. Forester looks at them and says, "Already? We haven't even got out of the county yet." Tara and Tina giggle, and Forester shows his soft side for these two special girls. We find a house not far off the highway and we stop. First the mandatory sweep for zombies, then we can relax.

No problems in or out around the house. We get in and the girls head two different directions. I remind them just because we haven't seen anything doesn't mean they can just go wherever. I make them stay together even for the "potty" breaks. They complain, but comply. I look around for Forester, and find him outside by the SUV. The look on his face speaks volumes. He lets me know that he has a bad feeling. Like something nagging at the back of his skull. He wants to get out of here and on the road now. I ask him what it is, and he says it's like we're being watched. Now I get nervous. The girls come out, thank God, and then a bullet passes by my head into the tree we're parked by. No thought, we get in and leave. The girls duck down crying as I aim the M16 out the window as a bullet takes the side mirror off the car. We speed out leaving a trail of dust to cover us as we flee.

Forester looks at me and says, "What the hell? Whoever that was could've taken us out at any time. What were they doing?" I don't have an answer. I'm just glad we're fine, and I'm glad to finally be on our way to the border.

We make it to the border between Washington and Idaho. We step out of the car completely speechless of what we see. A concrete fence, twenty feet high with barb wire on the top. Forester led us to a part of the border away from any metropolitan areas, but we still come to this. I wonder if it stretches across the Canadian border, or even the Oregon side. We approach a gate, wearily. There haven't been any deaders for a while, but that doesn't mean anything. As we step up to it, a crack of a gunshot and a small plume of dust rises from about ten feet away. We stop cold, and Forester is ready for anything. None of us brought a weapon of any kind, so we find ourselves at a disadvantage. A bull horned voice draws our attention to a guard tower I didn't notice before. There is actually one tower every ten to fifteen feet. "If you attempt to come any closer to the blockade, we will open fire," the voice says, At the top we see at least thirty guns pointed at us. Seeing as how none of us are lacking in common sense, we stop. "We aren't infected," I yell back, "we have two girls with us. Please, can't you at least take them?" "I'm sorry," the man replies, "Anyone in the quarantine zone is considered infected, and trying to leave will be stopped with lethal force!" Forester yells back, "We have information about a vaccine for the virus, you prick! At least let the girls-"another gunshot silences him down. "Hold your fire! Hold your fire! Look, we are under orders. Give me the information and I'll relay it to my commanding offi-" Forester replies with an unapologetic F-bomb, so writing that will not happen.

I tell them of the scientist in Winlock, and his mailing of the components of the vaccine. The soldier informs us that all mail state wide was stopped on or about May 10, when word of the virus got out. The border was sealed in about four days after that. There Is no way anything was shipped anywhere to contain the outbreak, he says. Forester lets loose another bomb and Tara repeats it. I look at her and she quickly mouths a "Sorry."
The scientist lied. Why? Is something happening back in Winlock that he wanted us out of the way? We need to go back. I was hoping that at least the girls could get out of this mess, but that isn't going to happen. I tell Forester, and he agrees. He is hoping the scientist is still alive, he says, "Cuz I'm going to kill him." I don't try to dissuade him. I'm not sure I can stop him even if I wanted to. We tell the girls, and they take it surprisingly well. I do over hear something that chills me to the bone. "Know what, Tara?" Tina asks, "if Forester doesn't kill that guy, I'm going to." "I'll help," Tara responds.

I really hate what this world is doing to these two innocent girls

14 A.V.

      I am going to need to find some more note books or something to write on. This is the last page in this one. We are currently in Spokane, Washington. Our vehicle broke down when we got here due to something getting into the engine. I am certain it is the deader we hit a few miles back before we got to town. I was driving while Forester rested in the back seat, Tara right next to him. Tina and I were talking when I looked toward her for a second and the deader came out of nowhere. We went right over the top of it and it made a loud thump underneath. The noise was enough to jar the sleeping two. I told them what happened, even though they didn't need my explanation. The deader left quite the smear on the windshield.

      The hotel we found to stay is quite big. Lots of empty rooms, a pool, and even an arcade. Not having any quarters, the girls are out of luck there. We are on the fourth floor facing downtown, so we should be able to see anything out on the road. Our rooms are right next to each other with a door between, and that makes the girls feel safe. I told them again, if one wants to go explore, do not go anywhere alone. Tara questioned why Forester and I can, but I remind them that I really don't. Forester, on the other hand, I think explains itself.

      Forester told me that he only checked the first few floors, and cleared out any "undesirables." He wants to check the rest of the upper floors, but after a good night's sleep. We both warn the girls to stay on the first four floors, and if they see anything, whether it is deaders, people, or something not right, to get back here as fast as possible. They agree.

      Since we are close to the fence surrounding the state, I'm going to leave this little "Dead Notebook" where I hope someone will find it. Hopefully, the military will begin a sweep of the cities looking for survivors, and try to bring the state back to what it once was. I think we are going to work our way back to the Winlock area. Except we're going to take a different route. As hot as it is right now, the fall and winter is coming, and I would like to be on the other side of the Cascades before either one hits. If anyone finds this, please deliver it to somebody of importance to keep anything like this from happening again. I have seen firsthand the level people have sunk to, and it is literally hell on earth. I don't wish this on anyone.

God bless
Hal Jones

To: General Thomas Samuels
Joint Chiefs of Staff
United States Army

From: General Thaddeus Morganstein
Department of Defense
United States Marine Corp

Tom

      A group of Marines was sent in to Winlock, WA, to secure the building we believe was where the D.A.V. was manufactured. Out of the eight that went in, three made it out. I am fairly certain they were unprepared for what happened. The survivors did recover a journal written by Dr. Mentler about his experiments, and the resulting disastrous results. I have included it for you to review, then we can plan from there.

Ted

From the journal of Dr. Darbus Mentler
2:45 A.M. PST
Winlock, WA
Feb 26

    The building we've set up the lab in is in a perfect location. Though the town is rural, it does have just about everything we may need. Plus, being right off the freeway, and only an hour's drive from Joint Base Lewis Mchord, is extremely helpful. There is also the big "Wally's World" less than five miles from here for any incidentals. The four soldiers that are staying with me for security have set up the equipment, computers, and even our living spaces rather quickly and efficiently. The General picked the right group for this assignment. They are also trained in the use of the computers and necessary biological research we are doing. If you can call it that.

    The General has also supplied us with a variety of small dogs and cats for our experimentation. I'm not happy about this, but it is for the greater good. At least that is what he says, but I wonder. What we are doing, I believe is illegal, but the General says not to worry. He cleared it and we have immunity. Although, something doesn't feel right about conducting the experiments in the middle of a town, no matter how small. Especially in our own country. But, like he said, if we don't do it, someone else will.

    The big picture? After what happened at the CDC, I should be happy to be working. I just pray that we don't get found out. Which is odd that I would pray being an atheist.

    I think I'll get to sleep, and begin work in the morning. Then I think I'll find the closest liquor store to get myself some "medicine".

February 26
Day 1
11:15 AM

I have made the decision for my own personal reasons to log, time and date everything I do. Partially to keep track of any progression in the experiments, but mostly to keep my sanity for what I'm about to do. Something isn't right, but I'm too committed to back out now.

Certain viruses I'm using are extremely volatile, and contagious. Even the air in the room I'm in is toxic to anyone who enters it without the proper PPE. I'm certain this has been planned before the General approached me. An airlock, fume hood, and incinerator are already in place for what we are about to do. Either he has a lot of fore sight, or he is nuts. Probably both, but I'm digressing. The first "concoction" I'm producing has within it a sample of the "swine flu", rabies and a strain of the Ebola virus. Thankfully the hood is here, for most of the work. Putting the proper amounts into the container, I will centrifuge them for the next twenty minutes for the proper a mixture. Or, what I determine is correct. This is a new form of science, creating this virus. I am actually intrigued at what it will do, but I'm also concerned. I guess I'll go pick my first subject.

12:03 PM

I've chosen one of the kittens, and it certainly is friendly. Very cute too. I feel bad for what I'm about to put you through, little one, but hopefully it will be short lived. Time to inject.

12:11 PM

It lasted a total of eight minutes from injection to the final breath. Looked extremely painful for the cat. I will now perform an autopsy to see the results.

1:20 PM
The results are inconclusive, but this is just the first try. Reviewing the video footage, I noticed something that I didn't see while conducting the experiment. According to the equipment, its heart actually stopped four minutes before it completely stopped moving. Looking at the internal organs, they have just about liquefied which probably killed it. I mean stopped it from moving. Even though its heart stopped, it continued to function for a few minutes. Is this what the General wants? I think I'm going to ask for some rats when I check with him in a few hours.

3:15 PM

The puppy that I'm using now is not happy. With last mix, I have added the avian flu, a stronger strain of rabies, and then some virulent streptococcus bacteria that introduces a form of necrosis. I believe. I'm going to place the dog with another one in a secure cage, and monitor the progression of the disease.

3:28 PM

I have set up special cameras and bugging devices around the building to watch the soldiers while they watch me. I overheard one of the privates say he was going to town to get some "strange stuff." I remember what that is, and I'm not happy. One of the reasons this particular private was "deployed" with me is because of his problem causing at the post. Plus, the assault charge from a female officer, but that was unsubstantiated. I will be watching him. He might be the lucky one to be my first human test subject.

4:17 PM

The puppy is starting to respond to the injection I gave him. He is acting listless, and he is suffering from a fever. He is also acting extremely agitated toward the other dog in the cage with him. That one is actually trying to hide in a corner. Interesting. After an hour, symptoms start to develop. I hope the general is happy.

7:42 PM

The subject has died. But, he is starting to move. The other dog is barking and whimpering, knowing that something is wrong. This will be fascinating.

8:15 PM

As hard as he could, the second puppy tried to fight him off, but failed. The first dog has begun to eat the other. This is unprecedented. A synthesized virus has not only brought a dog back to life, but turned it cannibalistic. The best part is this is only the first day. Now I know the General will be pleased. But, is what I'm doing right? Something tells me no, but this is very exciting.

Feb 28
Day 3
9:15 AM

I forgot to document yesterday. But the results were so amazing that I didn't know where to begin. I placed the infected puppy with an even bigger dog. But the bigger dog was scared to death. It barked and barked at the small dog, but it kept coming at the larger dog. The puppy was like a small pug, but the virus was changing it. Necrosis was manifesting on its right side as it lumbered closer to the dog. This dog was a German Shepard, and it was so scared it defecated. The puppy bit its leg, and the dog howled. Then whimpered as it tried to escape. It scratched the walls, jumped, whatever it could. The pup got a hold of it again, ripping a huge chunk off the tail eating it.
Utterly fascinating!

11:47 AM

I return to the Shepard and the pug. The pug is torn apart by the bigger dog, but the small one is trying to still get to the Shepard. The larger dog is panting, barely breathing. Within 5 minutes it is dead. I leave to attend to my report to the General. I'm very interested to see what happens next.

12:43 PM

The Shepard is walking around the cage. Absolutely remarkable. The creature was clearly dead. No doubt at all of the status of the animal. The pup is still trying to move across the floor, but only having one front leg, and being ripped in half puts a damper on its intentions. The Shepard though is eye-balling me with a very disturbing glare. I believe it is looking at me like I'm its next meal. Fascinating. Though it has a lumbering gate, it has run into the side of the cage several times trying to get to me. The only noise it can make is a raspy growling. The dog has lost the ability to bark.

The ramifications of what I'm trying to do at this time are unprecedented. I can't imagine what will happen to me or the General if his superiors find out about what were…I mean I…am doing.

March 17
7:08 Pm
Day 20

    A major problem has occurred. One of the soldiers has brought a young lady here for activities that I certainly do not approve of. These men are not taking the security of this facility seriously. Bringing this girl who doesn't look like she is even in her twenties is appalling. My experiments are much more important than their need for "release". If the General happens to show up unexpectedly, the man who brought the girl will probably be shot. As I walk through the lab going over my data, I hear a scream that freezes my blood. The girl has seen the German Shepard lumbering in his cage. The girl is quickly ushered into a room with the door shut and locked. I chastise the soldier for leading her into classified areas of the building. Realizing my mistake, I remember that the entire place is classified. I make a decision that I will regret for the rest of my life.

    I order the other 3 service men to lock the other one into the same room as the girl. They leader of the group, a sergeant, asks me what my intentions are. I inform him that my orders are not to be questioned. This individual broke protocol bringing the girl in, and I know for a fact that the General would call this treason. The decision I make involves using the two locked in the other room for human trials of the virus. The girl can never leave this facility, and the soldier will pay the ultimate price for his transgression. The remaining soldiers, except for one, inform me that they will not participate in this action, they are going to stop it. The sergeant, the one soldier who didn't object, pulls his side arm and shoots both in the knees and Achilles' tendon, completely taking away their ability to walk. They are screaming uncontrollably causing the German Shepard, and the puppy, to become agitated. The Shepard is slamming itself against the sides of the cage trying to get to the two soldiers. I shiver at the noises It is making.

10:17 PM

    I'm not happy with what just happened. The sergeant said he was acting under orders knowing that should something happen he was permitted to take whatever action necessary to defend the integrity of this project. I do admire his dedication, but I have to wonder what he was offered to be this way. But I can't worry about that right now. I go into the room where the dogs were, and I remember why I didn't keep a record over the last almost 3 weeks. The setbacks I had were very discouraging, and I almost gave up. Although looking at the dogs, I'm convinced the virus I developed will make the General happy. The necrosis on the dogs has taken almost all the hair, and some of the internal organs are hanging out of the holes in their flesh. I'm calling it a night. With the other soldiers locked in with the girl, I'm afraid of what the sergeant will do to me if I decide to do something that he feels the general wouldn't like. Tomorrow, I'm going to have to decide whether I want to continue with this project. I hope I can sleep.

March 18
7:15 AM
Day 21

    I wake up to something disturbing. I hear one of the soldiers who was shot is moaning in the infirmary not far from my quarters. I approach so that the sergeant doesn't notice me because what I'm hearing chills the marrow in my bones. The sergeant is explaining the necessity of patriotism, loyalty and other nonsense he isn't even practicing himself. I cautiously work my way to the control room where every room is under surveillance. The other soldier is strapped to the gurney we brought in. I watch as he puts together a syringe of the virus we injected into the test subjects. He turns to the wounded man, with a grin that would make the devil scared if I believed in such a thing. He puts the needle into the neck of the other soldier, and he screams. His face turns beat red as he starts to convulse. The sergeant lifts the soldier and carries him out of the infirmary to the make-shift "brig" the other prisoners are in. I can see through the cameras through-out our facility. He pulls his weapon as he unlocks the door and opens it. Pointing the gun at the others, he throws the soldier in. The others yell to be released, but decide that the crazy sergeant is not worth dying for. He shuts the door, locks it and precedes to come….oh my word. He is coming here. I have to get back to my room.

9:46 AM

    I'm putting some notes into my personal notebook when the sergeant comes into my lab. He wants me to follow him to the surveillance room. It wasn't a request. I remind him who is in command here. And I will be reporting this to the General when we have our next conversation at 1300 hours this afternoon. I think that is maybe 1 o'clock or something. I turn to my work to continue, but the hammer click of his weapon makes me stop what I'm doing. Looking his direction seeing the gun pointed toward me changes my mind about finishing what I was doing. We head to the monitor room.

9:53 AM

    We view the one soldier who wasn't shot trying to help the other the sergeant brought back to the make shift holding cell. The young lady is cowering in a corner. She looks as though she hasn't stopped crying for days. The other wounded soldier is just sitting in the opposite corner barely able to keep his head up. I am certain his life is about to end. Shortly, the other wounded boy, the one who received the injection drops his head down. Even in the monitor room his final breath is so audible he sounds like he is right with us. The non-wounded soldier bows his head, and he begins to shake. I watch him put his hand upon the eyes of the one who has passed and close them. The man stands, with tears in his eyes comes to the camera. I can feel his anger, hate, rage, through the monitor screen. The girl joins him as they both start screaming at the camera. I look to my side and see the sergeant smirking, then laughing at the tirade of the two. I look from him feeling the anger toward the person next to me that the other feel. I look back to the screen and I see the impossible.

    Never would I have thought my research, my work would make happen what I just saw. The dead soldier stands, and limps toward the screaming two. The girl notices, by some 6th sense something happening behind her. She turns, and barely gets out of the way as the dead man lunges for her. She inadvertently knocks the other soldier to the side as the dead one hits the wall. The two quickly move to the other side of the room as the dead soldier turns clumsily after them. The other wounded one starts to moan, and the attention of the dead soldier is turned to him. He lumbers to the wounded, outstretched arms, and mouth wide open. He falls on the incapacitated one, and I hear a scream that will haunt me to the end of my days. The other two in the room are in shock. The girl screams again, but in utter horror. The sergeant turns the camera to the dead and wounded soldier and laughs. The dead soldier is….is eating the other. I watch in complete disbelief as I see flesh hanging out of his mouth, blood running down his face as he chews.

    Nothing in the universe keeps me from recalling my morning meal and expelling it onto the console that monitors the events. Fortunately, my vomiting ways causes the console too short out, and we are spared the rest of the scene. The sergeant in his fury hits me and I fell to the ground. He leaves me to see in person what his work has accomplished.

    What have I done?

10:36 AM

    I have recovered the best I can from the sergeant hitting me. My nose isn't bleeding as much as when he struck me, but the grogginess from the strike is still there. I work my way back to my quarters to rest. No sign of the man as I walk through the building which make me breathe a sigh of relief. I enter my room and quickly lock myself in. There are a lot of things to consider when I contact the General today. I'm going to rest for now, and hope that the sergeant is too preoccupied to come looking for me.

3:15 PM

    My rest turned into a few hour long nap. I wonder if maybe I have a slight concussion. Damn! I missed my afternoon update with the General. I will have to try later.
    I look out my window at the quaint little town of Winlock, Washington that we have set up our little experiment, and I lower my head. What we...what I have done is inconsolable. Not only have I violated every ethical rule creating this microscopic monster, I've ruined any chance I had to hopefully go back to the CDC and continue my work. Word of this will get out. I have no doubt in my mind. I must do what I can to contain the virus here, even if it means terminating all the subjects. Including the unplanned human ones. I better start making plans because after I do what I'm planning I don't believe I will be able to live with myself. I hope ending my life will make some atonement for what I've done.
    I surprisingly still haven't heard from the Sergeant. I thought he would come looking for me for whatever twisted reason goes through his deranged mind. I should be ready for that also.

March 24
10:00 AM
Day 27

    I have no idea what is going on in the rest of the building. I haven't been outside in weeks, I haven't heard from any of the surviving soldiers, and looking outside it is surprisingly quiet. Considering the rain coming down, I'm not surprised. I see a family walking down the street coming from a pawn shop. Parents, two girls and a boy leaving with something I can't quite make out not that it matters. What matters is they look happy. I watch them wave to another young couple as they hurry to get out of the rain. I really do like this town a lot. I could retire here when the time comes. It isn't so small that everything shuts down at 6 o'clock, but it doesn't have the hustle and bustle of say Olympia or Tacoma.

    Enough day dreaming. I decide to step out to see what is happening with the rest of the people here to make a determination on what to do next. I make my way to the "brig" to check on the "prisoners. The door! It is wide open with no signs of the individuals! I cautiously look in to see blood. Everywhere. In one corner I see half a hand resting with what I think is a liver. I leave immediately finding the nearest toilet. Finishing that, I continue my search. The cages where the test animals stayed are empty! No sign of forced escape. They were released. I run to the rear entry of the building, and the door is wide open! Oh my god.

    I need to make a call.

10:12 AM

    I spoke to the general. He is an arrogant, obnoxious, evil son-of-a-bitch. I find out his plan was to do this the whole time. He planted the sergeant. Apparently, he is dying from some disease that the general neglected to mention when he introduced me to these 4 soldiers. Is the sergeant contagious? Are the other 3 infected by whatever disease he has? I don't know. Instead of producing a virus, I could have been working on a treatment, maybe a cure, for the sergeant. Instead, this egotistical bastard decided a weaponized virus was the best form of deterrent for would-be attackers and potential enemies of our country. Never mind the fact that biological warfare has been illegal for years. I hope the general is infected with his own virus, except that it causes him more pain than ever imagined by a human being. If he were here, I would end his life. I would go to the proper authorities and turn myself in. Even if it meant my execution.

    The perimeter alarm is going off. Someone or something has made entry into the building. I better find myself secure area, and a gun of some kind. It could be one of the test subjects, or the infected soldier.

    It's neither. The sergeant has come back. It also looks as if something has taken an enormous bite out of his arm. And shoulder. And leg. But he seems cognizant and aware of his surroundings. He has found me in the lab which fortunately has a secure lock from the interior, and extremely thick, bullet proof glass. He stands before me, looking guilty, but relieved that the disease he has isn't going to be his death. No, just something worse.

    He then tells me his story.

10:38 AM

      A few short months ago, he was diagnosed with and extremely aggressive form of AIDS related cancer. Not being one to pry, I decide not to inquire how he got it. I do, however, ask him if it was a manufactured. He says no. He doesn't go into details, but he does imply that his lived a promiscuous life style that was very open. I tell him to say no more about how he lived. It doesn't matter. I ask where he received his current injuries. He released the 4 prisoners before the infected soldier was able to assault the young lady and uninjured man. They ran out as the dead walker followed them. The girl screaming seemed to attract the infected man. At this point he can no longer be referred to as a soldier.

      The uninfected couple proceeded to leave the building. But two bullets ended their chance of escape. The infected stooped over the 2 and started to rip them apart and eat them. According to the sergeant, he was able to lure the man outside the building where he left the premises. He then dragged the other 2 outside placing them into a vehicle where he took them some place to "drop" them off. His departure wasn't long, so when he returned he let the test animals out of the cages. Luring them outside, they too proceeded to head out into the town. The sergeant said that he turned his head for a split second. Which was long enough for the Shepard to turn back around and attack him. Three times it bit into him, before he was able to shoot the dog in the head. The animal quickly died for the second time. This time not getting back up. That will be something to remember if and when I'm ever attacked by the walking dead.

      The sergeant looks toward his weapon, then to me. "Make sure the general knows I've done my duty," he says. I will never forget that because not 1 second later he put his 9 mm hand gun to his head and pulls the trigger.

April 22

I have no idea what time it is, nor do I care. I have secured the building after cleaning the mess the sergeant made after his undignified departure. I am not recording anymore work. No more tests, experiments, anything. The military left enough supplies to last for months amazingly enough. Solar power, coupled with a sufficient water supply means I could stay here as long as necessary without any issues. The worst thing right now is seeing what my handy work is doing to the town. A car not far from here has rolled. The driver still alive, but not for long. A group of infected have pulled him from the wreckage tearing him to pieces. His screams, along with everything else I've done will give me nightmares until I die. Try as I might, I can't kill myself. I'm not strong enough. Or weak enough. All I can do right now is watch this place destroy itself. I thought I saw some soldiers, but I might have been mistaken. I'm going to a store room to sleep. In there it is quiet so I can't hear what is going on outside this building. Which is the only good thing going at this time.

April 25

Will wonders never cease. I was contacted by the general who informed me that a company from the post will be down to begin operations to cease this madness. The madness is his. There is no stopping what has happened. Guns can't stop the dead, unless bullet goes through the brain. I believe a blow to the head could stop the dead, but I'm not confident. I do believe that the military will fare as well as a group of toddlers trying to work out quantum mechanics. It won't matter. Through the last few weeks to secure my place I have set up safeguards around the building. Not mines or explosives, but things that make substantial noise to draw the dead to unwanted visitors. I do think though, if I see the family, or the couple, I saw weeks ago I may let them in. Their joy just being with each other gave me hope. Something I don't have right now.

I decided to look over my notes. I don't know why, I just felt the desire to see where I went wrong. Oh my word. I completely forgot something I did in the beginning stages of the testing. I must go to the upper floor.

I totally can't believe I forgot what I did. I created an anti-virus (that's what I'm calling it) to the dead raising virus. The supplies are limited, but giving an injection will keep the dead animating virus at bay. Like a flu shot! The test kitten I injected with the anti-virus was left up on the upper floors. I then gave it the other virus and all it got was sick! It was totally fine after about 3 days! I have a cure! But I can't let anyone know about it. Yet. I will send a message to my brother in Montana. I'll send him the composition, and notes on how to produce it, but I'll keep some here on this floor where I did experiments that I wanted to keep quiet. The kitten is happy to see me. How nice. I'm going back to the lab to figure out what is exactly in this and produce as much as I can.

My return to the lab, I look out the window. I have to wonder why the power and such is still on. There is something else going on here that doesn't make sense. But I can't think about that now. I have to start working, and get a message to my brother. The military will be here any time, and I don't want them to hold the world for ransom with this vaccine. I know the sergeant got hold of all my records and forwarded them to the general. Well that won't be a problem now.

To: General Thomas Samuels
Joint Chiefs of Staff
United States Army

From: General Thaddeus Morganstein
Department of Defense
United States Marine Corp

Tom,

    The following information found in the notebook left by Dr. Mentler mentions the anti-virus he produced. We are currently in route to Montana to locate his brother. Small problem, his brother has a different last name due to their mother marrying again after the death of Mentler's father. The last name was, believe it or not, is Smith. It would almost be funny if the actual fate of the entire country wasn't at stake.

    On another note, we are currently receiving reports of a train going through the eastern part of the state every 10-27 days. The companies stationed on the Idaho side have heard the horn blaring at odd times of the day and night. As soon as we can start gaining a "beach head" from the security wall, and starting heading west, we will find out if this is true.

    I will personally be heading out to the Washington/Idaho border in about 4 days to survey the situation.

Talk soon,

Major General Thadeous Morganstein,
    D.O.D., United States Marine Corp

Chuck Singleton is the writer and cover artist of this story. His home is in the Pacific Northwest with his wife Amy and 5 kids. As of this writing, during the current situation in the state of Washington, his whereabouts and that of his family are unknown.

Made in United States
Troutdale, OR
11/21/2024